CONDEMNED BEAST

SAMANTHA BARRETT

Copyright © 2023 by Samantha Barrett, in Australia.

All rights reserved. No part of this publication may be reproduced, stored or transmitted in any form or by any means, electronic, mechanical, photocopying, recording, scanning, or otherwise, without written permission from the publisher. It is illegal to copy this book, post it on a website, or distribute it by any other means without permission.

This novel is entirely a work of fiction. The names, characters, and incidents portrayed in it are the work of the author's imagination. Any resemblance to actual persons, living or dead, events or localities, is entirely coincidental.

Jaye Pratt asserts the moral right to be identified as the author of this work.

Designations used by companies to distinguish their products are often claimed as trademarks. All brand names and product names used in this book and on its cover are trade names, service marks, trademarks, and registered trademarks of their respective owners. The publishers and the book are not associated with any product or vendor mentioned in this book. None of the companies referenced within the book have endorsed the book.

Second Edition.

Cover - Designs by L.M

Editing - Elizabeth Gardner

Formatting - Jaye Pratt

WARNING!

This is a dark retelling of the Disney classic, names and locations have been changed to fit the story.

This book contains scenes of degrading, spitting, forced proximity and content that may disturb some readers.

If you are ready to have the Beast tear your heart out and treat you like the dirty prey that you are, then turn the page!

For my Kimmy,
I adore you, love you and appreciate everything you do for me, the kids and Mark.
I love you, Kimmy, I am so glad I met you because I wouldn't have been able to do the fucking things I have without you.
This one is for you my Botox ride-or-die bitch.
Love you xx

CHAPTER ONE

BLAST

Standing here in the center of this godforsaken church has anger thrumming through my veins. I hate this fucking place! But it is the only place someone like me can live, huh, what I do daily isn't living it's... existing.

Father Cogsworth made sure that my existence in this place was unpleasant. Any time I would step out of line, I was met with the bite of his Roman scourge whip—my back is a masterpiece of scars from that fucking thing. Most of my body is disfigured from his beatings. See, this isn't like most churches where you drop a child off that you don't want expecting it to be raised right until they find a loving family No, this place is somewhere you send children to disappear. Father Cogsworth never banked on me growing up to become smarter than him. His first downfall was allowing me free reign of Lumiere Library. This place may be a shit hole but it has the best library in town as it holds all the knowledge and secrets of the most powerful men in the world.

"Sir?" I turn around to find Mrs. Potts standing off to the side in the doorway to the kitchen. I may be unwanted and unloved but her, Chip and Father Maurice are the only three people that have ever shown me any type of kindness. She smiles kindly, her gray hair is tied in a bun atop her head, she wears a maid uniform when she isn't even employed here but she just never leaves. Her eyes shine with love each time she looks at me. I don't understand it, I'm a monster, scarred beyond repair and full of so much hate I have no room for love inside me. "Your breakfast is ready. Would you like me to bring it to your office?"

"Yes," I grit out before marching to the opposite side of the church. I stalk up the winding staircase as I head toward my office on the second floor. After I *disposed* of Father Cogsworth, I took over the church and all its dirty dealings. The bastard would preach about welcoming God into your heart and ridding yourself of the darkness yet he was the keeper of the devil himself. I push my office door open to find Chip dusting the bookshelves. At the sound of my approach, he flicks his gaze to me and immediately bows his head. A growl slips from my lips, annoyed by his constant need to bow. "Stop fucking doing that!" I snap at the young kid, who like me was dropped at the doorstep of Lumiere but unlike me, he was raised by Mrs. Potts who loves and cherishes the boy.

"Mother would tan my hide if she caught me looking directly at you." I slam my eyes closed and take a deep breath to try to calm the anger brewing inside me.

"Fine. Go get me the blueprints of the city. I want every scrap of information you can find on the Amorro family." His eyes snap to mine, the shock in his gaze tells me the little shit has been listening in on phone calls and conversations he shouldn't have been. I narrow my gaze at him.

"Y-yes, sir." He quickly scurries from the room as his mother walks in with a frown marring her weathered face. She gingerly places the tray piled high with food in the center of my desk. I turn away from her and peer out the stained-glass windows behind me. I hate the fucking pictures in the glass, a man on one side, a woman on the other and in the middle pane they are together. Love is weakness.

I wanted nothing in life until I found that fucking mirror.

"Her engagement has been announced, sir." The hesitancy in the way she says that shows me even though she tries to act unaffected by my appearance, she isn't immune to the sight of me. I keep my gaze focused outside the ugly windows, the rose garden visible through the light-yellow colored glass. My garden isn't like most. We don't have red or pink roses, we have black and deep purple roses. The black signifies the color of my heart and the purple represents the colors of the scars that adorn my back.

"Good." Her gasp has me rolling my eyes.

"Sir, if you don't complete this then everything will be lost to her father." I spin around so fast, she stumbles back a step at the look on my face. I place my palms flat against my desk and glare at the old woman.

"Her father will die," I say without remorse.

Her brows furrow. "If she marries Gatson, then all will be lost. Everything you have ever wanted will be gone, your family name will be lost." I grind my teeth to stop myself from lashing out at her. She may speak the truth but that doesn't help the current situation we are in.

"Leave me!" I demand. She bows her head and briskly exits my office, closing the door quietly behind herself. My anger wins out, I swipe the tray full of food from my desk roaring out my rage. "Fuck!" I yell as I drop in my leather wingback chair, resting my head back. I close my eyes and try to escape my inner thoughts. I know what I am owed, it's all rightfully mine. Phillipe Amorro is a murdering bastard. He may have faked his way to the top, killed the previous Don in his way, but not even he is exempt to the old rules of the original families. Every daughter of a Don must pay a debt to the church of Lumiere. They are to remain within the confines of the church for three months prior to their wedding day, learn from the library about all the family traditions. I own the only library in the world that holds the history of all the crime families in the world.

"Beast?" I snap my eyes open to find Maurice and Chip standing in the open doorway. I scowl at them, annoyed I didn't even hear the door open.

"What, Maurice?" The old man wears a red cloak over his bullshit priest uniform, the sight of that white collar fills me with bitterness. Cogsworth knew who I was the moment I was dropped at the doorstep, he used me to try and secure his place in this fucking church. Maurice though, he never laid a single hand on me. He was the one who tended to my wounds with Mrs. Potts, that is the only reason I allow him and her to remain here.

"We found something," Maurice says as Chip rushes forward, laying the large book in front of me, neither of them commenting on the mess I have made. Chip points to a section in the book. I take a calming breath before leaving forward and reading.

'If the intended shall fail to marry their chosen, the heir to the prior don will be accepted as a replacement. The intended must decree in front of the old families, the new, their intended and the prior heir.'

I snap my gaze to Maurice. "Has this ever happened before?" He shakes his head.

"No, never in the history of all the families has an intended bride ever pulled out of an engagement." I narrow my eyes at the old man.

"Why?" I grit out. He squares his shoulders, lifts his chin and holds my cold stare as he answers.

"No one was ever stupid enough to leave an heir alive before." That has my brows raising to my hairline. I hear the truth in the old man's words. Maurice is a lot of things but a liar isn't one of them, he will always tell the truth even if it hurts.

"Bass." I snap my gaze to Chip and narrow my eyes, the little shit doesn't fear me like the others and it both pisses me off and brings me a semblance of... comfort. "You need to read this," I grit my teeth as I look down to where he is pointing.

'The intended may never be swayed by the previous heir, all must be the choice of the intended. The heir may never reveal who they are or which family they belong to. From the moment of the lockout the clock will start, allowing the intended three months to change their mind.'

I lean back in my chair and link my hands together as I stare at the two men in front of me. "So, when the pampered princess arrives for her lock out, she can never know about the heir we have in our clutches and we only have three months to convince her to change her mind without outright telling her why she needs to change it?" Chip cringes but nods. Maurice stands tall and holds my gaze as he speaks.

"It must be her choice. She has to want it and demand a change of partners on the night of her wedding." A dark smile breaks across my face.

"They said we couldn't tell her but, they never said we couldn't hurt her." Maurice pales, Chip drops his gaze to the ground as I slowly stand, feeling giddy for the first time in my life. "Get her room ready and hide any of the books that tell her too much and have them moved to my wing. She is to stay out of the west wing, if she is caught she will be punished!" They both nod. This is perfect, we have three months to work the girl, she is the last fucking chance we have.

"We may need to bring the groundskeepers back and some of the staff to make this place fit for a lady." I scoff.

"No, Maurice, she will see this place for what it is."

A fucking prison.

CHAPTER TWO

BELLA

Three days later...

"It's only a few short months before we can finally be together without stolen moments here and there, my love." Gatson's words should fill me with hope and excitement but they do neither. I tear my hands from his hold and spin away, moving toward the large bay windows that overlook the beautiful garden below. I love gardening but father never allows me to tend to the roses, he says that type of work is beneath me. If I wish to do something useful with my time I should learn to cook, clean or *service* my future husband. The thought of *servicing* Gatson has a shudder running through me. Don't get me wrong, he is kind and generous most of the time and better to be around then other men my father surrounds himself with, but there isn't that... *spark.*

"I don't want to do this," I say softly. I hear him come up behind me. He plasters his chest against my back—I've read plenty of romance books so I know him being this close should set butterflies a flight inside me but he doesn't. I don't even feel the need to melt into him and allow his warmth to put me at ease. He grips the sides of my arms and rests his chin atop my head.

"I know it will be hard being apart but we will get through this. I promise you, Isabella, upon your return you will have my sole attention and be my only focus." I fight the eye roll that wants to break free when he grinds his erection into my lower back. What he means is *I'll stop fucking anything with a hole because when you get back, I can finally fill yours.*

"Mistress, your car is ready." Grateful for the interruption, I pull free of Gatson's hold. I smile up at him before placing a quick kiss on his cheek and scurrying from the room. I follow Linda toward the front of the house ready to get the hell out of here. Gatson thinks I don't want to go because I'm scared and I'll miss him. That is not the case at all. At our approach Louis, our butler, opens the front doors for us. Before I can take a step outside, my father's voice has me pausing.

"Isabella, a word." I take a deep breath before slowly turning to face my father as he descends the grand staircase wearing his Armani suit like a second skin. His salt and pepper hair is slicked back, his black mustache sits proudly atop his upper lip. I hate the dang thing. His dark brown eyes spear me with a warning, my father doesn't love me. He sees me as a way to unite two warring families—I'm to marry for peace not for love. He stops a couple feet away from me, running his disapproving gaze over my outfit. I went with a peach-colored blouse and black slacks that flare at the bottom, allowing them to cover the cream-colored four-inch heels I wear. "You are to study, learn all there is to be learned and come back with a better understanding of the families."

"Yes, Father." My job for the next three months is to learn the history of the families. Upon my return I am to recite the knowledge I have learned to the founding fathers before they will accept my marriage to Gatson. If I fail... I shut that thought down as I hold my father's gaze. "I won't fail you, I will make you proud." My words seem to put him at ease a little.

"Good. If you fail, the demise of our whole family is on your shoulders." I bite the inside of my cheek to keep from snapping at him. As I nod and prepare to turn away, he reaches out and grips my elbow in a punishing hold. I grit my teeth through the pain, that is going to leave a bruise. His eyes bore into mine, I see the warning in them. "You are to keep your legs shut for the next three months. The only one who gets to ram into that cunt is Gatson." My nostrils flare as anger surges inside me but, like the good girl I have been raised to be, I smile and nod.

"Of course, Father. I have saved myself for Gatson even though he has fucked his way through my friend circle." The words fly out of my mouth before I can stop them. The moment his eyes narrow, I know I fucked up. His hand cracks across my face like a whip. I drop to the marble floor like a sack of shit. I hear Linda gasp but she would never step out of line and help me. I fight through my tears and bite down on my tongue as I push to my feet, nod respectfully at my father, then turn and make my way to the waiting car. My cheek burns but I refuse to give him the satisfaction of cupping it through the pain.

I peer out my tinted window as we come to a stop in front of wrought iron gates that look new. But it's the two letters in the center that capture my attention *B.V.* I furrow my brow, I was told that I would be coming to the Lumiere Library to study. A feeling of unease prickles the base of my neck. As the gates open slowly, the car lurches forward and slowly makes its way through the strange place. It's surrounded by nothing but woodlands, the road wasn't even marked that led us here. All around as far as the eye can see is gardens. I squish my face against the window as I peek outside, gasping at the sight of black roses. The car comes to a halt and I don't even bother looking to the other side where I'm sure the house is. My gaze is too focused on the roses. I shove my door open and stumble slightly as I get out. I ignore my driver's protest as I slowly move toward the bush.

The roses are blooming, God they are stunning. I slowly reach out to touch their petals. "Miss, no!" I yank my hand back and spin around to find a flushed young man standing mere feet away from me with a horrified look on his handsome face. I cover my heart with my hand and smile shyly at him.

"You scared me." A tinge of pink creeps to his cheeks, as a boyish grin breaks free and his green eyes shine with mirth. I look him over and furrow my brow. He wears old jeans that have clearly seen better days, his navy shirt is dotted with spots of bleach, his blond hair is tied back in a low ponytail.

"You must never touch the roses." His tone holds a warning.

"I wasn't going to cut them or anything," I defend. His eyes crinkle at the corners as his shoulders hunch slightly.

"The Master doesn't allow anyone to touch his roses." I frown expecting him to tell me he is joking but when he just motions for me to follow him, I realize he isn't kidding and the roses are really off-limits. I lift my gaze to what I thought would be a church but... it isn't. Maybe it was years ago but what stands before me resembles a castle!

It is huge. There are two towers on either end of the front. I see stained glass windows scattered everywhere, moss and vines cover the edges of the building. I've never seen anything like this before in my life. The castle has clearly been around for decades if not centuries, but no crosses can be seen at the tops of the towers or even above the main archway. "Miss?" I shake my head and quickly hurry after the young man who is carrying my bags, not sparing my driver a second look as I pass him. The moment I step through the huge wooden doors that look like they weigh a ton, I freeze, staring at a huge grand staircase with access on both sides, like only a proper castle would have.

There is a small podium at the base of the staircase but no pews. Doorways line the sides of the massive room, a large chandelier hangs from the ceiling, beautiful olden-day designs mark the marble floor beneath it. I chase after the young boy as he heads upstairs. We reach the second level and my eyes widen, paintings adorn the walls but they are destroyed with cuts through them all, almost like someone has taken a knife to them. I follow the young boy down a long, darkened hallway and frown. Do they not believe in lights? He stops in front of a set of double doors and uses his shoulder to push them open. He motions with his head for me to go first. I do as instructed and gasp.

"Holy shit," I whisper, ignoring the chuckle from me behind me as I take the room. A large four-poster bed with teal netting surrounding it. The large king size bed sits in the middle of the room. A large, beautiful wardrobe sits against the wall, white with gold trim. There are two doors off to the side of the room. I open one and marvel at the large walk-in closet. I open the next door and gasp. A large open shower with a rainfall showerhead sits at the other end of the room. A beautiful vanity with a large mirror against one wall and on the other side of the room is a huge claw-foot tub that would swallow my small frame whole. I turn around and watch as the young boy opens the two large windows either side of the far wall, then moves to the center. He draws the long net curtains back and opens the two glass doors to reveal a small balcony made of what looks like stone. "Is this where I'm staying?" I ask. He turns and smiles kindly.

"Yes. My name is Chip and I am here to help guide you and teach the rules of the manor." I hold in my scoff, this is no manor, this is a fucking castle fit for a king.

"What are the rules?" I ask as I place my hands on my hips and quirk a brow.

"You may roam freely throughout the manor and grounds but you may not touch the rose garden or go to the west wing." His tone holds a hint of a warning as he says the last part which just piques my curiosity.

"What's in the west wing?" I push, and the smile vanishes from his face. His eyes fall to the bruise on my cheek, I keep my gaze on his face acting like I have no idea what he is looking at. Truth is, I have become a pro at making excuses for the bruises that mar my body.

"It's the master's wing and is forbidden to you." The edge to his tone has me biting back my retort. "You are to be in the dining hall every evening for supper at six sharp, do not be late." He turns to leave but I stop him with my question.

"Where is the library?" He doesn't turn to look at me, just keeps his back to me.

"Father Maurice will be here to escort you there in an hour, please use that time to settle in." He doesn't wait for a reply, just closes the doors behind himself and leaves me alone in this strange room. I move toward the bed and run my fingers over the soft blankets. This place may look old and dusty but I can tell this bedding is new. This room looks freshly remodeled, the scent of fresh paint still clings to the air. No pictures or paintings adorn the walls in this room, it's bare of any personal touches. A gust of wind sends the scent of roses into my room. I smile and walk out onto the small balcony. I close my eyes and inhale the intoxicating scent of the flowers. I may be in a strange place but not living under the watchful eye of my father or his men has me feeling giddy and excited. I don't have to worry about Gatson showing up and demanding my time, I can just... breathe, well, for a short time anyway.

CHAPTER THREE

BEAST

I hide in the shadows watching her. Maurice leads her around the library showing her where everything is but she isn't focused on him. Her gaze is scanning every nook of this place. I watch as she reaches out to run her fingers along the spines of each book as she passes them, a smile plastered on her face. It's not forced, it's not even on her face for Maurice's benefit, it's there because it's real. She is genuinely excited and happy to be inside this impressive library that has been around longer than the city it resides in. This place is steeped in history, one thing Mrs. Potts always said to me was *knowledge is power*. She is right, the knowledge that I have learned over the years is the reason I am in the position I'm in now.

"Thank you, Father Maurice." The sound of her voice draws my attention to her mouth.

"You're most welcome, Miss Isabella." She tries to hide it but I see the sudden tension in her shoulders at the use of her full name.

"I was told Father Cogsworth would be the one teaching me?" Maurice gives nothing away as he smiles kindly at the girl and shakes his head.

"Father Cogsworth is away for a few months. Chip, Mrs. Potts and myself will be the ones teaching you all you need to know." Her little nose scrunches up as her brows draw in, and her hazel eyes narrow slightly—her long brown hair is plaited and falls to the center of her back. She pulls her gaze away from Maurice, looking right at me. My breath hitches but then I remember there is no way she can see me in the darkness. I cock my head to the side when I get a good look at her face, a bruise mars the left side of it. Darkness creeps into the corners of my eyes when I realize it's a handprint.

Who dared to touch her?

"Are there any nuns here?" she asks. I like how inquisitive she is. She keeps her gaze focused on me. If I wasn't shrouded in darkness I would swear she could see me.

"No, there are only four of us who remain here now." Maurice sounds bitter about that but it wasn't his call to make. No one outside of the four of us knows about Cogsworth's death and the lack of staff that exists in this place. She nibbles on her full bottom lip, she doesn't look like I thought she would. I expected a girl who was meek and unsure of herself, but Isabella Amorro doesn't display any of those traits, she oozes confidence and... sex appeal. I shake my head to rid myself of those types of thoughts, one look at me and she would be running for the hills.

"And they are..." She lets her sentence trail off, leaving it up to Maurice to draw a conclusion on if he will answer her or not. The old man adjusts his robe and pushes his lips to the side, clearly annoyed that she has backed him into a corner.

"Myself, Chip, Mrs. Potts, and the master of this... establishment." I nixed the use of calling this place a church the moment I got rid of Cogsworth. A church is a place to worship, forgive, and be free to believe in a higher power— this place was never that.

"And where is this master you speak of?" she asks as she slowly pulls her gaze from mine and faces the old man. Maurice tenses but keeps his face void of any emotion as he looks at Isabella.

"He is very, very busy and you won't see him for the duration of your stay." She rolls her lips over her teeth and nods. "I shall leave you to it then and fetch you in an hour before supper." He doesn't wait for a response, marching from the room exasperated after his small time with her. I shock the fuck out of myself when I feel a small smile stretch across my face. I don't fucking smile, ever.

"Here goes nothing," she mutters to herself as she heads toward a shelf Maurice pointed out to her. she runs her fingers along the spines and grabs out the books she needs before she carries them over to the little reading nook in the corner. She places the books on the table before sitting in the high-back chair and pushing her sleeves up. A frown forms on my face when I see yet another bruise on her elbow in the shape of a hand.

I've been leaning against the wall for so long my legs have gone numb, I don't know what it is about her that has me trapped in a trance-like state. She is beautiful, there is no doubt about that but she is also smart. I've watched her jot down notes on a pad, with a pen, I didn't even see her bring in, she reads aloud and I find myself being comforted by the sound of her voice and the way certain words roll off her tongue.

This is the only room in this place that brings me comfort. I love reading and have read almost all of these books. This library is like no other, this place has three floors full of books. I spend most of my time in here unless I have to work, I didn't know what the fuck I would do after Cogsworth was disposed of, then I learned the truth and everything fell into place. I had the money to keep this palace running. The sound of her ringing pulls me from my thoughts. She sighs as she reaches into her blouse, and my brows raise when she exposes the top of her right breast and I get a peek of a peach-colored bra. She pulls her phone from the cup of her bra.

"Great," she mutters before she answers the call, placing it on speaker and balancing it on the arm of her chair. "Gatson, what a surprise." The undercurrent of annoyance in her tone can be heard. I clench my hands into fists at my sides.

"I always love to surprise you, my love." She rolls her eyes at his words and I cock my head to the side, confused. The pictures I have seen of them together and all the posts on the internet suggest nothing but love and happiness. Seeing her now and the way she doesn't smile at the sound of his voice or perk up at him calling her, tells me that she doesn't love him. The internet is full of shit and she is a great actress for the camera, the look in her eyes now shows me she has desire to marry that bastard. That will make what we have to do so much easier. "Are you settling in alright?"

She crosses her legs under herself and places the book she is reading in her lap as she answers. "Yes. I'm fine, studying like a good girl and learning everything there is to know about the families so I can pass this test." The bitterness that coats her words has me believing that Isabella

Amorro is a great actress in the public eye, she even had me fooled.

"You will do amazing, I know you won't let me down." I can even hear the underlying threat in his voice.

"Of course not," she grits out bitterly. A feminine voice can be heard from the other end. I watch her intently to gauge her reaction, waiting to see a hint of jealousy. "Sounds like you have company. I don't want to hold you up."

"I have needs, darling. Once we are wed, I'll cut down on my *tastes*." A shudder rolls through her at the thought.

"Of course, speak soon." She doesn't wait for him to reply as she ends the call, a resigned sigh tumbling from her full lips as she closes her eyes and leans her head back. This woman is not what I expected and I can't decide if that is a good thing or a bad thing, yet.

Chip ambles into my office carrying a tray filled with my supper. He wears a bright smile as he places it on my desk in front of me. Normally he is eager to escape my presence but tonight, he stands opposite me, waiting. I roll my eyes and turn away from my computer screen to face the annoying little shit. I may be fond of him but that doesn't make him exempt from my temper.

"What do you want?"

He pushes his mouth to the side before sighing dramatically. "Would you care to eat in the dining room with *Bella*?" I frown at the nickname he has given her.

"Why the hell would I do that?" I snap.

"Because she is alone in this house like you, it might be

nice for the two of you to... hang out before everything blows up." I push to my feet, making Chip take a cautious step back and drop his gaze to the floor.

"Don't wuss out on me now. You clearly have a reason as to why you think *me* being near the heiress would be a good idea." He keeps his gaze on the wooden floor as he answers me.

"I just thought maybe if you... tried to let her get to know you things would be easier when the time came." I grind my teeth so hard they begin to ache. I lay my hands flat against my old wooden desk and lean over.

"Don't think, do as you are fucking told and keep her busy with the books."

"How is she supposed to learn everything if the key to all of this is in the books you have hidden in the west wing?" His backchat has me stumped for a split second before anger takes over and I lash out.

"Get the fuck out. You're not here to think, you're here to do as I say. I'll decide when and *if* she learns of this." His gaze snaps to mine, his eyes are wide with shock as he stares at me.

"You don't plan to take over, do you?"

"I have no need. I'm dead to the outside world so I don't see the point in a resurrection. She is the last daughter, so once she leaves, I'm free to seal the gates and never worry about any of this again."

"Beast, she is your last chance to reclaim what is yours. You aren't meant to spend your life hiding out here." I slam my fist down on the desk causing him to jump in fright.

"It's my fucking choice. Now, get the fuck out!" I roar. Chip drops his gaze and quickly scampers from the room.

I stand in the darkened corner of her room and watch her sleep. She looks peaceful. I wish I knew what that felt like—I've never experienced peace before. She rolls over causing the blankets to slip further down her body exposing her long tanned legs. Her silk bed shorts are fucking tiny, half her ass cheeks hang out the bottom, and the matching pink bralette she wears only covers her full tits and leaves the rest of her mid-drift exposed. Her long brown hair is loose and fans out around her. I itch to run my fingers through her locks.

I wonder what it would feel like wrapped around my fist?

I shake the thought away, she would never willingly submit to me and allow me to ravish her body in the way I want to. I'm no virgin, I've fucked plenty of whores, but I've never been with a woman who is willing to hand her body over without being paid. I doubt Isabella is any different. She turns again but this time she lays on her back, her parted legs causing her silk shorts to bunch to the side. I bite down into my bottom lip at the sight of her pussy. The moonlight gives me enough light to see her perfect pink lips, making my mouth water, begging for me to taste her. My cock begins to harden in my pants. A gust of wind blows through her open windows. She shivers, my attention is snagged when I see her nipples begin to harden and push against her silk bralette.

I scrub a hand down my face ready to flee this room and escape her intoxicating presence, but she speaks, halting me in my tracks with my back to her. "You're the master, aren't you?"

CHAPTER FOUR

BELLA

My chest is rising and falling at a rapid speed, and nerves thrum through me as I squint my eyes to make out the outline of him in the shadows. I could feel eyes on me all day in the library. Even as I slept, I felt the sensation of someone watching me which caused me to wake and see a shadow in the corner of my room. A normal person would have screamed but not me, I don't fear the monsters of the night. I know what real monsters look like and neither of them is here.

"Will you answer me?" I press, keeping my eyes on his back as I reach blindly for the bedside lamp.

"Don't." That one word has me stilling. The authority in which he says it has me wanting to obey. Normally, I would rebel against someone ordering me around but something inside me is telling me that this man isn't like any other, he would follow through on a threat he made.

"Okay..." I wait for him to turn around or answer my

previous question but he does neither. I attempt to slip off the side of the bed, ready to march over and confront him.

"Don't move." I huff out my annoyance.

"Why not?" I rebuke.

"Because you won't like what you see."

"Says who? You?" I push. I watch as he slowly turns his head to the side, thanks to the lack of lighting I'm unable to give any details or even tell you what color skin he has.

"You won't like it, trust me." The bitterness that coats each of his words has a pang of sympathy blossoming inside my chest for this poor man, he truly thinks he is hideous.

"I've seen ugly and believe me when I tell you neither of them is here." A dark chuckle comes from him. The sound of it has me sitting up straighter and almost begging to be able to see his face, so I know where that delectable sound came from. When the silence stretches again, I decide to push him for more. "Do you know why I'm here?" I watch him intently, waiting to see him shift or tense but he does nothing.

"Yeah." His deep baritone sends a shiver down my spine, the hairs on the back of my neck have been standing on end since I awoke. I had the same feeling today in the library. Who the hell is this guy?

"What else do you know about me?"

"More than you would like. Go to sleep, Bella, you have a lot of studying to do tomorrow." My eyes widen at the use of my nickname, but before another word can be uttered, he slips from the room, closing the door behind him. I tilt my head to the side, confused as hell at the strange encounter. There aren't a lot of *real* conversations I have had in my life. Most people fear me because of my last name. The others kiss my ass, hoping to get in with the family but no one ever speaks to *me*. Whoever the master is, he is the first person in my life to know exactly who I am and not give a shit about it. He spoke to me as a person, not someone he could use to gain a higher social status.

I'm woken by Mrs. Potts, who serves me breakfast in bed. I hate that she waits on me and helps me shower and change, I'm not incapable of doing things myself. People naturally assume because I'm a mafia princess that I can't wipe my own ass! I hate the misconception but I stopped correcting people years ago.

"Would you like some tea, dear?" Mrs. Potts asks me as I enter the library.

"Yes, please, and would I be able to get the WIFI password?" I ask as I take the same seat from yesterday, placing my pad, pen, laptop and phone on the table in front of me before looking at the elderly woman. I frown when I find her staring at me with a weird look on her face. "Is everything okay?" I ask, slightly weirded out by how intensely she is looking at me.

"You are so much more than I thought you would be. You may just show him that there is beauty in the world." I furrow my brow, thoroughly confused now. She doesn't allow me to ask her meaning as she turns briskly and walks out of the room, leaving me to stare after her.

She is a strange woman.

I open my laptop and use the hotspot from my phone to link it to the internet until I get the password. I begin to Google some of the notes I took down yesterday to get a better understanding of the meaning behind some of the words that were used. I give up using the laptop and go back to reading through the books, they are steeped in knowledge and hold so many family secrets I never knew existed. These crime families are not what they are made out to be, they have no honor or loyalty like they claim.

Well, some do, but most of the history documented here shows how families have turned on each other and wiped out entire families—even the women, children and the elderly aren't safe. When one family decides to eradicate another, they make sure your entire bloodline is gone, even if you're a second cousin twice removed you are slaughtered. But, the worst part to all of this is that all of the murders are made out to be accidental or done by a rival. The fact that the originals, or the elders as we call them, can't find proof means that no one has ever been dealt with for the crimes they have committed.

I've spent hours here reading, to the point that Chip has come to get me twice for supper but I refused. These books have me hooked and the need for answers is consuming me. I close the last book and blink a few times to let my eyes refocus. I frown as I look around and realize it's dark in here except for the lamp beside me. I stand and stretch, cracking my neck side to side to rid myself of the cramp. Not knowing where the light switch is in here, I grab my phone and use the torch on it to light my way back to the aisle to get more books. I need to find out what happened to the Vital family, but in order to do that I need to go back further to find out their history.

I shine my light along the spines of the books in the fifth row. I search the top and middle row trying to find the book marked Vital but there isn't one. I crouch down and scan the bottom row, when I don't see it the first time I scan it again and growl in frustration! I push to my feet and freeze the moment I feel a chest plastered to my back. My breathing picks up, my head begins to swim with ideas on how to make a quick escape but my body... it refuses to move.

I feel him lean forward and run his nose along my head, his scent engulfing me. Pine, mint and man. I don't need to see his face to know it's the same guy from last night. My body has a mind of its own and melts into him. I still, my eyes shooting wide. I have never and I mean *never* melted into Gatson or felt the overpowering need to have his hands on me, but with this wicked stranger, I am ready to feel his hands all over me.

"You look lost." The rich baritone of his voice has a shiver trailing down my spine and goose flesh erupting all over my body. I dart my tongue out to moisten my suddenly dry lips and swallow loudly.

"Uh, I... I can't find the book I need." I cringe at how breathy I sound but refuse to say more. A gasp tears from me when he grips my waist, his hands are so large they nearly wrap around me. He bends his head down, scraping his lips against the shell of my ear forcing a shiver to break free. I am ashamed to admit it but I can feel myself growing wet.

"Which book?" His husky whisper in my ear has me fighting back a moan.

"I need the book on the Vital family," I whisper, suddenly unsure on if I should be sharing what I am up to here, but last night he did say he knew why I was here. His grip on my waist tightens, not bruising but tight enough to let me know he didn't like my answer.

"Why?" His tone is harsh, but not angry.

"I need to brush up on the history of the families and... I need to know what happened," I answer honestly.

"The Vital family has nothing to do with your research.

They no longer exist and were wiped out before you were born," I scoff.

"They were murdered in cold blood twenty-eight years ago. How are they not a key piece to the families history?"

"You shouldn't go digging for the truth when it would show you how fucked up your own family is. Your father isn't the true Don of the families, he killed to become what he is." The venom that coats his words sends a tendril of fear shooting through me, for all I know he could be a creepy old man with a fetish for young girls.

"You speak about my family like you know us." My own voice holds an edge to it. I wish I could say I wasn't standing here equal parts scared and equal parts aroused.

"I know enough." He runs his nose along the column of my neck, a shameful moan slips past my lips. "You should focus more on the rise of your own family. There may be answers in there you never expected to need to know." I hear his words but they don't register straight away, thanks to the delicious sensations traveling through my body just from his touch and the feel of him pressed against me. "Go to bed, Bella, it's late." He places an open mouthed kiss against my neck drawing a loud gasp from me. By the time I am able to process what just happened, he's gone. I shine my light around me and race to the end of the row of books, but he's gone. Who the hell is this guy and what is it with him and hiding in the shadows?

After searching the surrounding rows, I decide to give up on trying to find the master of this castle and call it a night. I gather my things and use the torch on my phone to lead me back to my room. The entire place is eerily quiet, not a sound, except for the nighttime wind outside, can be heard. A place this size, I would expect it to be bustling with staff. Maybe I'm researching the wrong things, maybe I need to start researching Lumiere and what happened here. Something tells me that this place is full of secrets and in order to uncover the truth, I am going to have to break a few rules, like going to the west wing and see what lurks in the shadows.

CHAPTER FIVE

BEAST

This place may be old and withered but I did have it fitted with a few new gadgets like cameras. I can track her every move, like now how she pauses at the base of the stairwell that will lead her to the west wing, I can see the torn look on her face. She is thirsty for information but she is looking in the wrong places. She needs to not worry about the Vital family and focus on her own, how her father became the Don of one of the strongest families in the country. I watch as her shoulders slump in defeat before she carries on toward her room. I close the lid on my laptop and stare out the window of my room. The night is full of stars that shine so brightly they almost make you want to smile.

A knock sounds at my door. I call out to come in knowing it will be Chip. He is the only one out of the three of them willing to disrupt me when I am in my quarters. He cautiously enters the room and stops mere feet from the door. I narrow my eyes in warning, the only reason he stands that close to the exit is that whatever he has to say is going to piss me off and he needs a quick escape.

"Say it," I growl. He nods stiffly and focuses his gaze over my shoulder.

"I received a text message from Bella asking for any information on Lumiere." My brows dip as my eyes crinkle at the corners.

"What?" The quietly spoken word has him tensing.

"She said she wants to know what happened to... the master." His eyes slowly slide to mine. I can see he is trying to read me but I refuse to let him see my surprise. I knew our interaction would peak her interest but I didn't think it would be enough for her to abandon her study of the families and look into *me*.

"Give her the history of the place but nothing after Cogsworth took over." His brows raise in surprise, a small smile tugs at the corner of his mouth. "What?" I snap irritated.

"Ma had hoped she would pull you out of hiding and I think she may be right." I narrow my eyes, ready to tear him a new one but he's smart, he turns and literally runs from the room. Deciding that sleep won't be an option for me, I make my way out to my garden. Tending to my roses brings me a sense of peace, it calms the beast inside me. I grab a hoodie before I leave and take the back corridor like always. I know the others are used to the sight of me but I won't run the risk of her running into me. I pull the hood over my head and stuff my hands in the front pocket as I make my way down the spiral staircase that leads me to the kitchen. I don't stop when I see Mrs. Potts in there, I push through the back door and walk around to my garden. The moonlight lights my path, the stars are bright in the sky, the nighttime air is crisp, indicating that winter is near. Winter is my favorite time of year as I love the cold and enjoy the fact that you need to layer up which means I get to hide myself beneath layers, unlike in summer where everyone wears next to nothing.

I stop at the edge of my garden, close my eyes and inhale the intoxicating scent that these midnight roses give off. They smell the same as other roses but for me, the mixture of purple and black smells richer. Almost like the darker they are the stronger the scent. I never cut my roses. They may be trimmed, but only by me. I find caring for these flowers soothing, it helps me get out of my own head for a short while anyway. I spot my pruning scissors on the brick, I must have left them out here the other night. I grab them and go about my task of pruning back the leaves. I get so lost in my task that I don't register the shouts coming from her balcony. I hunch down and slink back into the shadows near one of the bushes and look up. She stands on her balcony, tense and clearly angry. She has her phone pressed against her ear, wearing the same sleep shorts and top from the other night. My eyes drink in the sight of her perfect body and unblemished skin, my mouth watering, wanting a taste.

"Angelina, I don't give a shit that you slept with Gatson but I do care that you're supposed to be my best friend and fucked him anyway." My eyes widen in surprise at that declaration. So she doesn't care her intended is fucking everything with a hole but she does care her best friend fucked him. Good to know. "Maybe I need to start fucking my way through his friend circle." I stand in anger, there is no fucking way I will allow her to fuck anyone.

What the fuck?

I have no idea where that came from but I don't care. I drop the pruning scissors and use the shadows to cover me as I slip around the back of the house where the power box is. I tear the cover open and kill the power, instantly I'm bathed in darkness. Maurice and Mrs. Potts won't bother to try to fix the blackout, they're used to me killing the power so I can hide in the shadows. It's how I've learned to blend into a room and use the shadows to conceal myself. Chip hates that I hide but I don't give a shit. I have no need to be seen. I make my way toward the stairs but halt behind the banister as I see a phone light coming from Bella's wing. I smirk, she isn't afraid of the dark, good, because you're about to have the darkest of sins inside you soon. I think to myself.

I watch her slowly make her way along the landing toward the library. I slip around the corner and head toward the supply closet at the back of the entrance. There is a staircase in there that leads you to the second story of the library. I know this whole palace like the back of my hand, I don't need a light to shine my way, darkness is my home. I push through the door of the second story of the library and quietly close it behind me. Well, the door is actually a bookshelf but who cares. The main door opens and I slowly slink forward and watch from my perch up here as she enters, closing the door behind herself. She shines her light all around, looking for what, I have no fucking idea. When she spins around giving me her back, her long hair swings with her movement and I itch to wrap those strands around my fist.

"I can feel the hairs on the back of my neck standing up, that has only happened three times, well four if we count this time." I bite my bottom lip and remain silent. "I know you're in here," she says as she slowly swivels around in a circle. I retreat backward and start to move along the stacks of books so she can't pinpoint where my voice is coming from.

"Then why would you come looking for me in a blackout?" Her sharp intake of air has my arrogance growing, this woman is a puzzle. Most girls would scream, hide and call for help but not her, why?

"I figured since you like the shadows so much this would be the perfect time for you to be out." I stop at the top of the stairs that will lead me down to her and can't fight the smile that breaks free. I watch as she takes a deep breath, squares her shoulders and looks toward the other side of the room, where she thinks I am. When she speaks, I use that time to descend the stairs. "Call me crazy but I have a feeling if I turn this light off, you might just appear." She clicks a few buttons on her phone and then the light is gone and we're bathed in darkness. I'm at her back within a second. A small chuckle escapes her the moment she feels me behind her. "You really do like the darkness, don't you?" I bend so my lips brush against the shell of her ear.

"I am the darkness, I'm your deepest darkest desire." A shiver rolls through her. She turns her head to the side but I don't move, with no light in here and my hood up she won't be able to get a good view of me.

"What makes you think you know what I desire?" She sounds almost breathless. I slip my hands around her waist, loving the gasp that slips free. I lay one hand flat against her stomach while I trail the other up and over her tit as I wrap my hand around her throat. She doesn't fight me, instead she leans her head back against my chest exposing her neck to me.

"You should be scared," I growl. Her lips twitch as if she wants to smile.

"But I'm not," she answers and I slowly lower my hand

from her stomach to the waistband of her sleep shorts and bend down, swiping my tongue along the side of her neck. Her mouth drops open and forms the perfect O.

"Why?" I ask as I nip at her neck and slip my hand beneath her shorts, then slowly lower my hand inside them until I'm cupping her pussy.

"I...Uh..." She tries to thrust her hips forward, but I tighten my hold around her neck to keep her still.

"Answer me, Bella." A moan tumbles from her full lips at the use of her preferred name. I slide a single finger through her folds and growl my approval. She is fucking soaking, the insides of her thighs will be wet. "Do you ever wear panties?" I rasp out as I bite down on her lobe drawing a loud moan from her.

"N-no." I close my eyes and try to tame the hunger inside me, she is perfection. "You intrigue me, I want to know more about you." Her honesty stuns me for a moment.

"Why would you want to know me? You have no idea who I am yet you seek me out and allow me to touch your cunt like I have a right." A whimper sounds out, causing my eyes to widen. "You like the kink of this, don't you?" Another whimper escapes her as I slip a single finger inside her tight wet hole—she's so fucking tight.

"Shit," she breathes out as she tries to raise onto her tiptoes. My grip on her neck keeps her in place as I slowly work my finger in and out of her taut virgin cunt.

"You like the thought of me fucking you and never knowing who I am, don't you?"

"Yes!" She answers honestly so I reward her by quickening my pace. "Oh fuck."

"Your pussy is clamping down on my finger so fucking beautifully, my cock is getting jealous."

"Oh my God." I bite down hard on the soft flesh

between her shoulder and neck in warning. She cries out but not from pain, Isabella Amorro is a dirty girl and is loving what I'm doing to her.

"God doesn't exist here, Bella, just the beast." Her only reply is to moan. She angles her face to the side looking up at me. Shock ripples through me when she cups my face through my hood and before I can register what is happening, she pulls me down to her and kisses me. My shock allows her the advantage of slipping her tongue inside my mouth, and the moment her taste hits my senses, a need so vile and depraved overcomes me. I deepen the kiss as I finger fuck her, refusing to allow her to break the kiss when she tries to, forcing her to moan into my mouth. I swallow each of her cries, loving the fact I am the one bringing her darkest desires to life. A mafia heiress like her shouldn't want such dark and depraved things, yet here she stands, with a man she doesn't even know with his finger buried in her cunt.

I allow her to break the kiss when I feel her body begin to grow taut. "Yes, you're gonna make me come!" I tear my finger out of her. "What–" She doesn't get a chance to finish before I'm shoving her forward to the edge of the table in the center. I bend her over the edge so she is face first keeping my hand on the back of her neck as I grip the back of her sleep shorts.

"Tell me to stop or I'm burying my cock inside your cunt," I growl. Need coats my words as my cock is rock fucking hard and aching to be inside her.

CHAPTER SIX

BELLA

I should be ashamed that I have just allowed a stranger to plunge his fingers inside me but I'm not. Something about this guy has me becoming a wanton slut. He brings my body to life even when my mind is screaming at me that this is wrong. If I allow him inside me and Gatson or worse my father finds out, I'm as good as dead. Marrying Gatson is a fate worse than death so if being here for three months means I can I finally allow myself to live out my fantasies, then so be it.

He grinds his hard cock against my ass drawing a moan from me—if he feels this big inside his pants, I'm scared to imagine how big he is when his cock isn't confined to his pants. "Answer me, Bella." The way he says my name, like he has every right, sends a shiver down my spine and need pooling between my legs.

"Do it!" Two simple words. That's all it takes for him to tear my satin sleep shorts from my body. I gasp, not in fright but from the need coursing through me and loving how he is just taking from me what he wants without a care in the world for who the fuck I am or who my father is. His hold on my neck is gone then both his hands are gripping my ass cheeks, squeezing them as he parts them. I feel a cool liquid slowly leak down my asshole and gasp, before I ponder that thought any further, I feel him drop down behind me. I turn my head to get a better look, but before I can see what he is doing, a cry tears from me the moment I feel his tongue push inside my pussy at the same time his thumb pushes inside my ass. I lurch forward on the table. He holds me in place as he pushes his tongue in and out of my pussy at the same time he fucks my ass.

Fuck!

"It's too much!" I cry out when I feel my orgasm cresting but this one feels different from when I use my rose vibrator, this one feels like it is going to tear me in half.

"Shut the fuck up and push that cunt back on my tongue. I want your come all over my face." Oh my God, his crass words have me obeying his command. I push back against his face, loving how his tongue slips inside my greedy cunt. His thumb is deep inside my ass, the feeling of having both my holes filled at the same time has me crashing. I scream at the top of my lungs when an orgasm so powerful tears through me, leaving me literally weak in the knees. I expect him to stop and shove his cock inside me but he doesn't, he pulls his thumb out and then replaces it with his tongue.

"Holy fuck!" I cry out at having the feeling of him eating my ass. God it feels so fucking good and I'm not afraid to admit that I reach back and grip the back of his head, holding him there as I ram my ass against his face, forcing him to continue to eat it. After a couple seconds he yanks free of my hold. I'm a panting mess and I can feel my wetness slowly dripping down my thighs. I've never been this turned on before in my life. I lay flat against the table panting and ready to beg him to make me come again if he doesn't fuck me in the next five seconds. The sound of a zipper being undone has me panting harder ready to feel a cock inside me for the first time.

"I'm gonna ruin you for anyone else." His whispered words have an edge. "I'm gonna break this cunt in nice and hard, then your ass is mine." A whimper escapes me when I feel the head of his cock slip through my folds. "I don't do slow or make love, I fuck ruthlessly. Last chance to back out." The grit in his tone tells me it may just kill him if I was to decline him right now, but saying no is the last thing I want right now.

"Fuck me, hard... Beast." A growl of approval sounds from him before his hand lands a swift smack to my ass, causing me to lurch forward and gasp. I don't get time to recover before he's doing the same to the other side, except a moan tears from me this time. My pussy clenches on nothing but air when he does it again. He massages my cheeks to soothe the ache before he lines his cock up with my hole and inches forward. I tense on instinct.

"Relax, it will hurt worse if you fight it." I try to do as he says and take a few calming breaths but it's fucking hard when he keeps pushing inside me and doesn't allow me to adjust or prepare when he slams the rest of the way inside me. Stars dance in my vision as a scream of pain tears from me. He slumps forward pressing his chest against my back. I feel his rapid breaths against my neck as I try to fight back the tears that want to break free. "Fuck, you're so fucking tight." Words fail me, I'm unable to speak through the pain coursing through my body. As if he can sense my discomfort he places a tender kiss on my shoulder. "I'll make you feel so fucking good."

Call me crazy but I trust him to come through on his word. He pushes back and grips my hips as he begins to move inside me, slowly. I grit my teeth and try to think of anything else except the pain. He slips one of his hands beneath me and begins to circle my clit, making the pain quickly bleed away to... pleasure. The feeling of him fucking me and toying with my clit at the same time has my body heating and I find myself pushing back against him needing... more. He is quick to oblige, his thrusts picking up in speed and intensity. I'm not expecting to come from an internal orgasm, I'm not naive enough to think I will be one of the lucky ones who can come from sex and not oral. He moves his hand from my clit and grips my waist again. He's fucking me so hard that the table skids along the wooden floor, as wanton moans tear from me.

"Fuck!" I cry out when he hits a sweet spot inside me that has me needing him to do it again. Which he does and my toes curl. He keeps to the same pace, fucking me hard and deep. I gasp when I feel a strange sensation brewing inside me, am I going to come? Just as the thought strikes me he slaps my ass and then I'm sent soaring. "Beast!" I scream as I shatter beneath him, screaming out a release so fucking strong and powerful that it has black spots dancing in my vision.

"Fuck yes, milk that cock for all it's worth, Bella!" My pussy clamps down harder on his cock. "Take it all like a fucking dirty girl." Powerless to him, I do as he says and take it all. I feel his cock beginning to swell inside me. A sense of pride overcomes me knowing that I am the one who is causing this beast of a man to fall apart. Before I can do anything, he's pulled out of me and then I'm on my knees in front of him with his cock right in my face. He pumps it angrily in my face four times before I feel the first spurt of cum land just below my eye. He throws his head back, roaring out his release as he comes all over my face. I kneel here in shock that he would do such a thing. My thoughts are cut off when he grips my hair in his hand harshly and presses it against my lips. "Suck it clean." I open my mouth to protest but I don't get the chance before my mouth is filled with cock. I have never had a dick in my mouth before, so I immediately begin to gag and choke on it. My mouth is stretched so wide I can't even swallow when he begins to thrust in and out of my mouth, the sounds coming from him telling me he loves the fact I am actually choking on his dick.

I grip his strong thighs and try to push him back but he doesn't budge. He pushes his cock so deep inside my mouth, I can feel him at the back of my throat. He yanks free and releases his hold on my hair. I slump froward on hands and knees gasping for air. I suck lungful after lungful of air, trying to regain my breathing and get myself under control. After a minute or so I finally manage to get my breathing back to normal and my heart rate back to a normal rhythm. I sit back on my haunches and find the spot in front of me empty. I frown as I try to see through the darkness where he went. I know he's still here because the hairs on my neck are standing on end.

"I'm sorry, that was too much." I turn the other side and squint my eyes hoping to catch a glimpse of him but of course, I see nothing. "Here," he says and something smacks me in the face a second later. I pull it away and try to figure out what it is but my lack of night vision doesn't help. "I destroyed your shorts. I thought you might want something to cover yourself with." My eyes widen, I realize it's his hoodie I'm holding. I manage to find the opening and slip it on. It's so big on me that the sleeves cover my hands and it falls to my knees. I shamelessly lift the collar to my nose and inhale, it smells like him which brings a smile to my face. "You should get some sleep, the power will be back on shortly."

My mouth hangs agape as realization dawns on me. "You cut the power?" I accuse. The deep rumble of his laughter has my breath hitching and my emotions running wild at the sound. I may not know who he is or what he looks like but there is a connection between the two of us, I can feel it. I guess the fact he hides in the shadows and I hide in plain sight makes us kindred spirits in a way—we both wear masks hiding our true selves from others.

"Had to get you alone somehow," he teases. Something tells me he doesn't smile or joke often which makes me sad.

"You could have just asked me." I smirk and feel the residue of his cum on my face. I cringe. "I need to go shower but... I guess I'll see you around?" I hate the hopeful lilt in my own voice.

"Really?" He sounds shocked.

"What?"

"Most girls would be screaming and cussing me out right now, why aren't you?"

I decide to answer honestly. "Call me crazy but that was the first thing I have ever done for myself and not because I was told to. I wanted it, you gave it so I don't see why I would be pissed at you?" It comes out more like a question than I would have liked but, oh well.

"You, Bella Amorro, are a mystery and I think I am going to like having you in *my* home for the next three months." I bite my lip to keep from smiling as I reach for my phone on the edge of the table. I hear him moving from across the room and say,

"I wasn't going to turn the torch on, I get it. You don't like the light or want to be seen with the heiress of the Amorro family. I respect that." A gruff sound comes from him, then out of nowhere I feel him at my back. He grips my waist and pulls me back against his chest. I admit, I melt into him and don't even put up a fight.

"The fact you think I stay in the shadows is because of you makes me want to laugh. If you knew who I was and what I looked like, you would be the one running from this place." The rawness in his tone has me feeling like that was extremely hard for him to admit.

"Looks are nothing but the surface we allow others to see. The soul inside you is what makes you beautiful." The sharp intake of breath from behind me, clues me into the fact he was not expecting something like that to come from me. I grip one of his hands from my waist and bring it to my mouth. It's rough and calloused from hard labor. I love that. I place a gentle kiss to the top of his hand and step forward out of his hold only releasing his hand at the last second. I keep my back to him even though every part of me wants to turn around and get a peek but I don't and that's only because I can still feel the ghost of his cock inside me. "Goodnight, Beast," I say quietly before slipping out the door. I swear I hear him whisper,

"Goodnight, Beauty."

CHAPTER SEVEN

BEAST

Maurice and I have been holed up in my office all morning. I didn't realize that Bella marrying Gatson impacted me so much until Maurice brought me some new information. If she marries and starts a new line with Gatson, all previous families must surrender their assets to the new couple and their families. That way they are able to divide the territories and delegate jobs evenly. See, this is what fucking happens when you have a greedy, power-hungry fucking Don as the head of the families.

"So, because he is Polish and marrying an Italian, that means there is a whole new line in the family mix, meaning what?" I question Maurice.

"Meaning, you cannot claim your birthright once the ceremony is complete. I don't believe Miss Amorro even knows she is in a lockout or that she has three months to find an heir to wed instead of her Polish fiancé."

"Fuck." I grit out as I lean back in my seat and glare at the stack of paperwork on my desk. Movement on the monitor snags my attention. I swivel around to get a better look. Bella is in the library but not sitting in her usual seat in the corner. She sits at the table I fucked her on two nights ago. I haven't gone back to her since then. I never should have allowed myself to touch her, but once I got a feel of her soft skin and the way she responded to my touch, then took everything I gave her and begged for more, had me powerless to say no.

"She can never know." Maurice's softly spoken words have me snapping my gaze back to him. He doesn't cower from the pressure of my gaze, he meets it head on. "You can try and act like you don't know what I mean but the girl has been wearing a hoodie five times her size to supper for the last two nights. Unless you have suddenly allowed her into the west wing, where she could have stolen it?" I narrow my eyes but the old prick doesn't care. Maurice and Mrs. Potts don't fear me. In their own fucked up way, they care about me and only want what is best for me.

"I don't know what you're talking about," I lie.

"Hmm." He molds his lips together as if he is deep in thought. "So you wouldn't happen to know how Miss Bella got that nasty love bite on her shoulder then, would you?" Fuck. I grind my teeth together trying to think of a plausible response but come up blank. "She is a beautiful girl." I shoot him a warning look that has him chuckling. "Son, I may be old and once upon a time been a priest but you and I both know it's been many years since Mrs. Potts slept in her own room."

I can't contain the laughter that escapes me. Maurice's eyes soften at the sound. "Touché, old man."

"Bass, she could give you everything you have ever wanted," he pleads.

"Why do you care so much?" My voice has an edge to it but he ignores it.

"Because, all he ever wanted for you was to grow up in a world filled with peace and love. That was stolen from you and I will forever regret my decision." He hangs his head in shame. I don't blame him anymore. He did what he thought was right and no one could have known how this would play out. "Give her a chance to get to know you. She may not know the laws of the families but she is a smart girl and will follow her heart. If she was willing to hand over her virtue to you and risk death if her father found out, that should count for something."

"What makes you think I fucked her?" He pins me with a dry look and shakes his head as he stands.

"My boy, blackouts only happen when *you* do it, meaning the house was dead silent with no TV's or air-con running to muffle the screams coming from the library." I bite the inside of my cheek to keep from laughing again. What the fuck is wrong with me, I never laugh! "Now, unless Miss Bella was reading some great books in the dark and... taking the edge off alone..." He leaves his sentence trail off as he leaves the room.

Six sharp is supper time, tonight I have something different planned. I instructed Mrs. Potts to have a lone candle lit at Bella's end of the table and to serve my meal at the other. It's an eighteen-seater table so I know for a fact she won't be able to see me. At six-fifteen, I flick the breaker off at the circuit board. I make my way back inside and just like I knew she would, she remains seated and continues to eat her meal like nothing is amiss. Her fork stills halfway to her mouth the moment I enter the room. Tonight I wear a pair of old jeans and another black hoodie with the hood up. She may be able to make out my silhouette but she can't see my features.

"Oh, so you are alive, pity." I push my tongue against the inside of my cheek to keep from laughing at the annoyance in her tone. I ignore her until I'm seated in front of my plate. I grab my knife and fork and just as I'm about to bring it to my mouth her words have me stalling. "Don't choke."

I smile around my mouthful of food and push out a moan just for her, the candlelight allows me to see the angry look on her face. "You seem annoyed?" Her eyes narrow but she says nothing then proceeds to spear her food and stuff her mouth trying to finish her meal quickly and escape me. She eats like a starved animal, once she is done she grabs her napkin and dabs the corners of her mouth before pushing back from the table ready to stand and flee the room. "Nice hoodie," I say when she stands.

"Well, I needed something big enough to shield me in case Chip decided my face or body was his to come on like someone else." The mention of Chip coming on her or even being near her has anger soaring inside me. She takes one step and that has me snapping. I swipe my plate and everything else in front of me off the table. She squeals in surprise.

"Get the fuck over here, now!" I snap. She raises her chin in defiance, causing my cock to harden inside my jeans. "Now, Bella!" She growls low in her throat before stomping toward me. She stops beside me, ready to have a go at me, but I render her speechless when I grip her waist and lift her until she sits spread eagle in front of me on the table.

"Hey–"

I cut off her protest when I strike out and clamp a hand around her throat squeezing just enough to show her who is in charge. "You ever fucking spread your legs for Chip and I'll kill him in front of you, then fuck you right next to his corpse."

She tries to pull free. I tighten my hold on her neck and grip one of her thighs in a punishing grip drawing a whimper from her. "You're fucking sick," she snarls.

"Hmm, let's make a deal then." She tenses.

"What deal?" Trepidation is clear in her voice.

"I'll let you go and never bother you again but–"

"But what?" she interrupts.

"You have to tell me that you're not wet right now."

"I'm not wet," she rushes to say.

I tsk her. "I never said you had to tell me with your mouth. Your mouth can lie but your pussy can't." I slip my hand from the top of her thigh and slowly slide it along the inside. Her breaths begin to become erratic in anticipation. The moment I reach the apex of her thighs and feel nothing but lace, my eyes shoot wide.

"I thought Chip might appreciate lingerie, don't you?" I growl, and release her throat, then use that same hand to shove against her chest until she is lying flat against the table. I grip her legs and pull her down until her ass is balancing on the edge. I grip her panties and relish in the scream of protest that comes from her when I tear them from her body. "Hey!" I ball them up and shove them inside her mouth, then cover her mouth with my hand when she tries to spit them out. Her arms come up to hit me but I grip them both in my hand.

"Keep your fucking arms above your head. That stays inside your dirty fucking mouth until I say." She tries to speak but it's muffled. She tears her hands from my hold and holds them above her head. I use my free hand to slip between us, cupping her pussy and she shivers. I slide a single finger through her folds and find her wet, just like I suspected. "You dirty little liar. You're fucking dripping for me, aren't you?" She whimpers in answer. "I'm gonna make you pay for lying to me but right now, I'm fucking starving and need to eat." Her eyes widen as I remove my hand and drop into my seat. She lifts her head and stares down at me. "Lift your legs and balance your heels on the edge of the table." She does as I say, exposing her fucking perfect pink pussy to me, even with no light I can see how she glistens. I part her folds with my fingers and swipe my tongue against her clit.

"Mmmmmm," she cries out.

"Take that shirt off, I want to see your tits." She scrambles to rid herself of the hoodie, then rests back on her elbows and I smirk. "You really wear no bra for Chip or for me?" I reach out and pull her panties from her mouth and stick them into my jeans pocket.

"Does it matter?" she sassily replies. I grit my teeth and shove a single finger inside her forcing her to cry out from the sudden intrusion.

"When it's my face you're about to ride and come all over, I'd say it does, don't you?" I say as I pump my finger in and out of her at a leisurely pace knowing it will be driving her mad, she bites down on her lip to keep from answering. I allow it, until I feel her pussy attempting to clamp down on my finger. I stop all movements and wait. She glares at me—but she can't see shit.

"Why did you stop?" The indignation in her voice has a dark chuckle coming from me.

"Answer my question or you won't be coming."

"You're joking?"

"I don't joke, Bella, not when it concerns whom this pussy comes for." I begin to move inside her again and she moans, she reaches up and begins to tweak her nipples. She tries to remain silent thinking I won't know when she is about to come but her pussy betrays her, she tries to clamp down again and I stop.

"Fuck!" she cries out when I deny her an orgasm again. "Fine, I wore the thong and nothing else for you, now please for the love of fucking Christ make me come before I cry!" Triumph surges inside me. I bury my face in her pussy and eat her cunt like a starved man. I know her excitement isn't just from her pending orgasm it's the voyeurism aspect—she's thrilled at the thought of someone walking in and catching me eating her pussy while she is laid out like a feast on the table. I slip two fingers inside her, she whimpers and tries to quieten her cries. It aggravates me that she is holding back.

I continue to pump my fingers inside her as I speak. "Stop holding back," I growl.

"The...God...others will...hear," she moans out.

"Let them!" I pull my fingers free and hold them out to her. "Suck them clean." I can't see the look in her eyes but I would imagine them to be wide with lust. She wraps her plump lips around my fingers and sucks them, making sure to swirl her tongue around the tips as she pulls back. I grunt my approval then reach down to unbutton my jeans, she snakes her hand out and grips my wrist earning a growl of disapproval from me.

"I...Can I?" she hesitantly asks, as she slowly lifts her gaze to mine, I nod my head stiffly and step back allowing her to slip off the table. She keeps her gaze down as she begins to undo my pants, then slowly pushes them and my boxers down my legs. What she does next I don't expect. I stare down at her as she slowly lowers to her knees, lifting her gaze to mine and I still. If I didn't know any better I would swear she was able to see me in the dark. "I've never done this before, well, except for the other night when you… ya know." I frown, surely I fucking heard wrong.

"You mean to tell me you've never given head?" She shakes her head. "What have you done?" She drops her gaze from mine and begins to squirm. "Answer me, Bella."

She keeps her gaze down as she answers. "Only what I have done with you," she whispers. My eyes widen as my brows hit my hairline. I knew she was a virgin but I had no fucking idea she was completely innocent.

"So, you've never been eaten out?" Again, she shakes her head, I scoff. "But you have kissed a guy?" When she doesn't answer I push on. "Right?" She slowly lifts her gaze back to mine.

"Only you." My sharp intake of breath is so loud in the silent room, what the fuck have I done?

CHAPTER EIGHT

BELLA

He stands there staring down at me with such intensity that I feel it deep in my bones. I was so angry with him for not coming to check on me the night after we had sex. I thought he would at least come to me last night but no, he just shows up during supper and expects to have me as his main course. I snort internally, who the hell am I kidding? I was hoping I would be the main course even though I was mad at him.

"Why the fuck would you let me do those things to you?" I can hear the anger that laces his tone. I feel him ready to shift and I just know he's going to flee so I do the only thing I can think of to keep him here. I grip his cock in my hand and hold him in place, the second I pump him a strangled hiss escapes his sinful mouth. I continue to pump him loving the sounds he makes, I stretch up on my knees and close my eyes praying that I do this right and don't fuck it up. I wrap my lips around the head of his cock and suck, hard. "Fucking hell!" He grits out, I immediately release him and drop back on my haunches.

"I'm sorry, I didn't mean–"

"What the fuck are you saying sorry for?" My brows draw in.

"I thought I hurt you or did it wrong," I answer honestly.

"You're hurting me now by not sucking my cock. Do that again and this time suck it as deep as you can." Pride swells inside me at his compliment. I must be sick in the head for his praise to mean anything to me. I've never seen his face or even know his name, yet here I am on my knees before him, sucking his cock as deep as I can. "Yeah, Beauty, just like that." His pet name has a moan slipping free from me. I feel a shudder roll through him. I can only take half of him into my mouth, so I use my hand to pump the base of his cock as I bob up and down on the head. The scent and taste of him is driving me crazy. I never thought sucking a cock would turn me on but here I am dripping wet to the point my thighs are slick with my own arousal. His hand fists the back of my hair keeping me in place as he begins to fuck my mouth, I gag around his cock with spit dripping down my chin. I reach out and grip his naked thighs at the back. I feel uneven skin there almost like he has scars, my attention is pulled back to his cock when he shoves it so far down my throat tears instantly roll down my cheeks.

He yanks his cock out of my mouth and I gasp for air, he doesn't give me a chance to catch my breath before he is pulling me to my feet and bending me over the table like last time. He lines his cock up with my entrance, he doesn't push inside me slowly like last time. No, he slams inside me so hard I cry out in pain, tears rolling down my cheeks. He reaches down and grips the front of my throat using his hold to pull me up so I am flush against his chest with his cock buried deep inside me. He bends his down and licks the tears from my cheek, then places a featherlight kiss on the edge of my mouth.

"You." *Thrust.* "Never." *Thrust.* "Should have." *Thrust.* "Let me fuck you." He continues to thrust inside me, chasing away the pain and replacing it with pleasure, when his free hand reaches up to pinch my nipple I cry out. Fuck, having him finger fuck me and play with my nipples feels a thousand times better than when I do it myself. Something about handing over the reins to someone else and entrusting them to bring you pleasure is so... erotic and freeing. He releases my throat and drapes my arm over the back of his neck but his fucking hood is up, I want to shove it back and see him but I just know he would run. He keeps tweaking my nipple with his hand while he leans down and sucks the other into his hot mouth.

"Holy fucking shit!" I cry out. "Oh fuck yes." I don't know whether it's the fact his cock is hitting the perfect spot inside of me or that he is toying with my nipples that has me ready to tetter over the edge but I'm not going to last. "Kiss me." His movements slow for a beat and I worry he will deny me but when he releases my nipple and shifts his mouth to mine I don't close my eyes, needing to see his. He stops thrusting inside me the moment our eyes connect, I can tell from how pale his eyes are that they are blue but I don't dare shift my gaze from his. I need him to see that I'm not scared.

"I will destroy you," he says with a sureness that should have me running away, but I don't.

"I think you already have," I whisper against his lips. I don't want to think about what we are doing, I just want to *feel.* I smash my lips to his and close my eyes knowing that is what he wants, he wants to remain hidden and I'll give him that if he continues to fuck me like this. He slides his free hand down my body and lifts my right leg up so it balances on the table. I gasp into his mouth. He feels so much deeper from this angle, God it feels so fucking good. Slipping his hand around the front, he runs a finger up and down my slit as he fucks me. "Beast," I whimper as I break our kiss, the use of that name has something snapping inside him. He pinches my clit between his fingers and fucks me so hard I have no choice but to trust the hold he has on me to not let me fall.

"Come all over my cock, Beauty." His words shatter me. I come screaming his name until my throat is hoarse. I slump in his hold. he wraps his arms around me, keeping me in place as he chases his own release. "Bella!" he roars as he comes deep inside my trembling pussy. How he is able to remain standing and bear my weight as well as his own I will never know. I am utterly spent and boneless but in the best possible way. "Shit." His curse has me snapping out of my moment of elation.

"What's wrong?" I ask as he slowly pulls out of me. I flinch the second he is free, my vagina stinging like a bitch. He reaches down then grabs something, then tosses it to me. It takes me a second to realize it's the hoodie of his I was wearing, I slip it on over my tired body as he fastens his pants. I can tell something is wrong, he went from being attentive to wanting to break shit in the space of a second.

"I fucked up, that shouldn't have happened. That was careless and I'll take care of it first thing in the morning." He storms out of the room, leaving me standing here shocked, confused, hurt, and with his cum dripping down the inside of my thighs.

I stand under the spray of my scalding hot shower, mentally berating myself for allowing him to seduce me again. I don't know what it is about him but the husky baritone of his voice does things to me. Even the way he commands my obedience has a thrill zapping through my body. I sigh as I close my eyes and stand under the spray. Even with my eyes closed I know the lights have gone out and he's here. I don't even bother to move, what's the point? I take my sweet ass time showering in the dark, even though I can't see shit I want to make him wait and see how he likes it. I shut the shower off and try to reach for my towel that I laid on the rail next to the shower but my hand is grabbing nothing but air.

"Looking for something?" The humor in his tone pisses me off. I may have given into him easily earlier but not this time. I step from the shower and stand on the bath mat, not caring that water is dripping everywhere. I twist my hair and get as much water out before I march my naked ass out of the bathroom and ignore his outstretched hand with my towel. I head straight for the closet and bite back my growl, the light switch doesn't work which means I'm going to have to guess where my things are. I see his shadow from the corner of my eye in the doorway but ignore him as I reach blindly for something to wear. "You can keep trying to ignore me, but you will crack soon enough." I manage to find a pair of old sweats and mentally high five myself. I turn my back to him as I bend over and pull them on. The moment I stand tall I feel him at my back. I keep my breathing even as I reach out to grab a shirt but freeze when he reaches around me and cups my tits.

"Don't touch me," I grit out, the arrogant bastard pinches my nipples as he speaks.

"Don't be pissed at me." I scoff and try to wrestle free of his hold. He pinches my nipples harder drawing a yelp of pain from me. "Calm the fuck down."

"Why should I?" My anger peaks and I'm unable to contain it any longer. "You fuck me, disappear for two days, fuck me again and then tell me it's a mistake. What did you expect me to do, drop to my knees and thank you?" I snort. "From now on, you can go find someone else to fuck in the dark because I won't be used like a fuck doll again. I have the rest of my life to be treated like that and I won't spend my last months of freedom being that for you." No sooner have the words left my mouth, than he has me spun around and pressed up against the wall of the closet with his hand around my throat. I gasp, not from how he has manhandled me but from the fact he is right in my face and has no hood on. My eyes drink in the sight of his hair, it's long enough to grip and run your fingers through, the fact I can see it in the dark tells me he must be a blond. I run my gaze over his face and thanks to the moonlight I can see a scar that runs down from the top of his brow to beneath his eyes, another scar mars his cheek.

"Tonight wasn't a mistake, the mistake was me fucking you bare." I'm loathe to admit it but it takes a full minute for his words to sink in. I'm too distracted by his handsome face. "Are you even listening?"

"What?" His eyes narrow. "I mean, yes, I was—am listening."

"No, you're not." He releases me and takes a step back. I've never faced him front on like this, he is fucking tall. I'd say a full foot taller than Gatson. He has a wide build, call me stupid but I feel happy at the fact he isn't completely hiding in the shadows.

"I'm on the pill, you can chill out."

"You take the pill but you're a virgin?" he mocks.

"*Was*, I *was* a virgin until you fucked me over the table in the library." I watch as his teeth sink into his lower lip. Fuck, why won't he let me see him? "I'm on the pill because it helps slow the flow of my periods. Happy now?" I don't wait for a reply as I blindly grab the first shirt I touch and stalk out of the closet. I pull it over my head as I make my way over to close the curtains before I climb into bed. The ache between my legs is still present and now my nipples hurt thanks to his stupid hold on them. I snuggle into the covers and face the curtains giving him my back, hoping he'll take the hint to leave.

"I'm sorry," he says quietly. I can hear him getting closer to the other side of the bed but I refuse to acknowledge him. When I feel the bed dip on the other side I tense in anticipation. He leans back against the headboard but doesn't climb beneath the covers. I lay motionless waiting for him to speak, or do something. "I shouldn't have been so rough with you." The earnest tone of his voice is the only reason I roll over, I look up at him but can't see shit thanks to the curtains now blocking out the moonlight. He runs his fingers through my wet hair, it's strangely soothing.

"I liked it," I whisper into the still nighttime air.

He chuckles lightly. "I know. Like I said earlier, your pussy doesn't lie." He may not be able to see it but I feel the blush coat my cheeks. Hearing him speak like this, instead of in the heat of the moment, is so different. Now I just want to hide as the memories of what we did play through my mind. "Get out of your head Bella."

"Huh?"

He sighs. "I can hear you overthinking from here. Don't make what we did into something dirty and wrong."

I snort in disbelief. "Seriously? I have never seen you, I don't know your name, or anything about you for that matter. You tell me not to make it dirty yet it is. I am literally fucking a stranger!" My voice rises slightly but I don't care!

"Fine. Let's play a game, a truth for a truth?"

CHAPTER NINE

BEAST

This is a huge risk but I also know she is right. I need to give her something in order for her to trust me. I'm not ready to end this. I fucking crave the feel of her and I admit, there is no way I would be able to keep my hands off her for the remainder of the time she is here now that I have had a taste.

"Okay, how do I know you are telling the truth though?" she asks.

"How do I know you won't lie?" I retort.

"Something tells me you already know everything there is to know about me. I'm also not dumb enough to think that you sleeping with me doesn't give you some type of an advantage over my father." She couldn't be more wrong. Sleeping with her has nothing to do with her father, it does however have everything to do with her.

"Your father means nothing to me. I don't care what Phillipe–"

"The fact you know his name tells me more than you think." She sounds bitter.

"You forget where you are, Bella. You came to Lumiere to learn the history of the families. Of course, I know who your father is. Who do you think he spoke to when organizing your stay here?" I feel her flinch. I'm not lying, well I am a bit. Maurice actually spoke to her father and arranged this. I declined her stay but as usual, Maurice went behind my back thinking he knew what was best. He may be right this time.

"I didn't think of that," she says quietly, not wanting to dwell on her father and risk my temper spiking for what he did. I should hate her on sight but I never project hate onto anyone unless they do something to earn that hatred.

"Why did you let me fuck you?" She tenses briefly before slowly relaxing. I keep running my fingers through her wet hair. She is a stubborn little shit, that's for sure. I like that she doesn't give in.

A whoosh of air escapes her before she finally answers. "My whole life, I have been told what to do, what to wear, how to speak, my life has never been my own. Coming here is the first taste of freedom I have ever had. I've never done anything like *that* before in my life. I guess a part of me wanted to do something for myself."

"Why?"

She tsks me. "No way. My turn, why won't you let me see you?" I expected this question but I didn't expect it to be so hard to answer.

"Like you, my life was laid out for me from the moment I was born. When I turned eighteen, I found something in the unlikeliest of places that granted me my freedom from the horror I was living in. For eighteen years of my life, things happened to me that made me the way I am. I don't live in the darkness because of me, I do it because people don't understand what they see when they look at me."

"Fuck them." The conviction in her tone has me looking down at her. She shifts and rests her head in my lap and throws her arm over my thighs. This type of touch is fucking new to me. I've never cuddled, or held someone before but now, and I feel compelled to. "If they want to judge you, let them. They are narrow minded fucks that probably jerk off to their own pictures." I splutter, shocked to hell at her words. Within a second the both of us are laughing, it feels strange hearing that sound come from my own mouth.

"Do you want to marry Gatson?" She sighs.

"No. I've never viewed Gatson as more than a pain in my ass. He says he loves me but he's full of shit. My father wants this marriage because he says it will bring peace to the families." I grit my teeth to keep my retort inside me, the lying fucker. He wants this because it means he inherits everything from all the other families. "If I had a choice, I would marry for love and because it's what I want not because it is expected of me." The solemn tone of her voice has me wanting to offer her a way out, except I can't. If I do that I will lose everything, despite how I treat them I could never do that to Maurice, Mrs. Potts or even Chip. "My turn, how old are you?"

I can't help it, I fight back a smile and keep my voice as even as I can. "Forty-three." She leaps off me so fast I can't hold my laughter back even if I wanted to.

"That's not funny!" she abolishes me. I can't even speak because I'm laughing so hard. I haven't laughed like this in... ever. It takes me a couple of minutes to get myself under control. I grab her and place her back in the spot she was before she freaked out. She tries to fight me but we both know I'm stronger and not above forcing her to do as I say.

She huffs out her annoyance but lays her head back in my lap as I continue playing with her hair. "You're joking, right?"

"Yes, Bella."

"Thank God, how old are you and don't joke around."

"I'm twenty-eight." Her whole body relaxes at my answer.

"Thank fuck," she mutters.

"Not into the daddy kink? Daddy's like to spank their naughty girls," I tease.

She snorts. "Nah, I have a daddy to smack me around without fucking me." My hand stills in her hair and my whole body tenses beneath her.

"The bruises on your face and arm, your father did that?" I growl.

"Now you see why I can't say no to marrying Gatson." White hot rage burns inside me. That lowlife scum had laid his hands on her. I don't realize I've wrapped my hand around her hair and begun to pull it until she yelps.

"Sorry," I grit out as I release it. "Why do you stay?" My tone has an edge to it, she either doesn't notice or just ignores it.

"I don't have a choice. I tried to run once when I was fifteen. He found me within an hour and believe me when I tell you, the pain was not worth it."

"Your father is a cunt, no man should ever lay his hands on a woman."

"I recall you smacking my ass." Her words help to lighten the mood slightly. I grin as I tug on her hair lightly eliciting a small laugh from her.

"I *recall* your pussy squeezing the life out of my cock as I did it and don't pretend you didn't love it, your puss—"

"Yeah, Yeah I know. *Your pussy doesn't lie.*" Laughter bubbles out of me hearing her trying to mimic my voice.

"Smart ass. Do you like studying about the families?" I ask to distract myself from thoughts of fucking her. I'm already sporting a semi just from hearing her say the word *pussy.*

"Yeah, I actually do. I find the history fascinating, there was so much loyalty between all the families years ago but now, the word family doesn't even seem to fit." Truer words have never been spoken. "I found something interesting though."

"What did you find?"

"Something happened nearly thirty years ago, but in order to understand what that was I have to go back further." She sighs. "Lucky I still have months left or else I'd be screwed." The thought of her leaving here has me feeling... lost. "My turn, will you tell me your name?" I take a deep breath, I promised not to lie but I also can't tell her the truth.

"My name is Bass but no one calls me that."

"I like it, I think it suits you." We keep the questions light and easy, spending hours asking each other things that we like, and what would be our dream jobs. I've never given much thought to my life, I always just lived day to day. My life is a series of events since I took over from Cogsworth, I don't plan to make it to my thirtieth birthday. With what I have set in motion, I don't see a way of me coming back. When the sun begins to rise she finally falls asleep. I stare down at her and marvel at the natural beauty. With Bella, her beauty isn't just on the surface, her true beauty radiates from inside her. She is kind and genuinely just wants what is best for everyone.

I slowly slip out of the bed and stare at her sleeping

form, she looks so peaceful. A pang of regret hits me in the chest. I wish I could spare her feelings when all of this comes out but I can't. She's better off away from her family, away from all this toxic shit and even though it pains me to admit it, she's better off away from me as well. Quietly I slip from her room and head toward my wing, I need to get my head on straight and not let her cloud my judgment.

"No hood?" I pause just outside Chip's room where he leans against the frame with his arms crossed and a smirk on his face.

"Mind ya fucking business," I growl, grip the hood of my hoodie and pull it up.

"It was meant as a compliment, Bass, you should wear it down more often," he says before retreating inside his room and closing the door. I march to my room and throw the door open. Pissed off, I yank the hoodie over my head and practically tear the shirt from my body in a fit of rage. I storm into my closet and stand in front of the mirror that changed everything. This old antique mirror held something greater than its age. The silver edges have green vines woven into the sides, black roses dot the edges of the oval shaped mirror. At first glance it just looks like an old mirror. I only found the truth when I accidentally knocked it off the wall in Cogsworth's office. I found everything I needed behind the glass. I had it fixed a couple of years ago, I hate mirrors but I just can't seem to let this one go

I stand here and stare at myself. My blond hair has tinges of brown through it, my lips are full and plump, my blue eyes are bright but full of self-loathing. I have a scar that runs from just above my eyebrow to just below my eye, another scar lines the side of my face from Cogsworth using his letter opener on me. I run my gaze over my naked torso and immediately I'm filled with disgust, my chest is marred with scars that can be seen through the tattoos that I got to cover them. They are large and protrude on my skin. You don't even have to look hard to see them. I turn around and look over my shoulder at my back, a masterpiece of torn skin. I refused to cover these scars with tattoos. These scars serve as a reminder of why I am doing this, why I can't let go of my father's legacy. My arms are covered in tattoos, the scars on them are nowhere near as bad as my torso. He never struck me where people could see unless he was in a blind rage.

I shove my pants down and glare at the scars on the backs of my thighs. I've learned to be ashamed of my scars. They are a reminder that I'm not like other people. Fuck me. My neck is even tattooed all the way around to hide the rope marks from when he would drag me around. I'm a horror movie brought to life. I pull my pants up at the sound of approaching footsteps and step out of my closet to see Maurice standing in the doorway of my room. His eyes are on the stacks of books in the corner.

"She is going to realize they are missing," he says.

"She doesn't need to know shit about that family," I snarl as I head for my bathroom to splash my face and brush my teeth.

"Her own family is represented in those books. She needs that history or she will never pass." I splash some water on my face before turning to Maurice.

"She won't need to pass. I plan to end her father before the wedding." Maurice's eyes snap wide.

"That is a suicide mission—"

"What the fuck would you have me do, old man?" I yell. "I'm caged in this fucking place because of what I look like and who I fucking am. I shouldn't exist, Maurice. If they find me then I'm dead and so are all of you. I'm a heartless cunt but not even I could let the three of you die for me."

His features soften as he takes a step toward me. "I don't want that life for you. If you do this there will be no more shadows for you. You will be at war with the Polish and in broad daylight."

"I know." A heaviness settles on my chest. "We have been working toward this for years and now is the time. Even if she doesn't claim the heir, she still deserves her freedom and if me doing this will ensure that, then that is what I will do." Maurice's face hardens.

"If you do this, I'm planning it. We have networked for years under their nose and amassed the numbers that we do have. I'll warn the founding fathers an hour before. You cannot kill the elders Bass, they must be spared." I hold his gaze so he can see the seriousness in my eyes when I say,

"If I find out any of them knew the truth and had the proof, they will die."

"You know one of the founding fathers is her grandfather?" Chip and I found out months ago that Isabella's grandfather is one of the elders. Her mother's father was elected when his daughter married Philippe. What we don't know is if he is fond of his son-in-law or not.

"I don't care. If he gets in my way he's going down with that cunt. They took my life from me and now it's my turn to take theirs."

CHAPTER TEN

BELLA

I wake around noon and cringe. I have missed breakfast and lost a lot of study time. I make quick work of changing and fixing my hair before I make my way to the library. The moment I step through the doors I blush at the sight of the table. Last night is a night I will never forget. We spent hours talking, getting to know each other. Some of the things I shared last night I have never told another soul, there is just something about Bass that makes me feel like I can trust him. He told me stories of his childhood. I know he watered it down for my benefit but I appreciate the fact he even shared anything at all. I know he isn't used to talking, he said so himself last night. I shake myself from my thoughts and take my seat at the table where I left the book I was reading yesterday.

I left my laptop, pad and all that in here, not wanting to carry them back and forth each day. I cringe when I see I forgot my phone here last night. I take a deep breath and pick it up. I fight another flinch when I see all the missed calls and messages from Gatson and my father. I ignore Gatson as I quickly dial my father. He answers on the fourth ring.

"Where the hell have you been?" I pull the phone back from my ear so his shouting doesn't blow my eardrum.

"Sorry, father, I was caught up studying and didn't—"

"I don't give a fuck. You are to be reachable at all times." I grit my teeth and take a calming breath.

"Yes, father, it won't happen again," I push out in a sickly sweet voice. I've found it's easier and saves me a lot of pain if I just stroke his ego and agree.

"Good. Now, Gatson wants to push the wedding date forward and I agreed." My breath lodges in my throat, my heart sinks and my stomach begins to swirl in the space of a second. My head grows dizzy. I knew it was coming but I guess I had lulled myself into thinking this was all a dream. "Do you understand?" His angry tone pulls me from my inner turmoil.

"Sorry, father, the line was distorted," I lie. He huffs out his displeasure.

"You will marry Gatson, two days after you arrive home. No sense in waiting the three weeks. The man wishes to return to Poland as soon as he can and you will not fuck this up. You will pass that fucking stupid test or so help me you will beg for death." He doesn't wait for a reply, he ends the call and with that, any hope I had of this being a bad dream. My chest feels like it's caving in, my head continues to spin. I drop my phone to the table and grip the edge to steady myself. I lean my forehead against the cold wood as I close my eyes and try to compartmentalize everything I am feeling. I'm normally really good at not feeling things and being able to hide my emotions, but marrying Gatson is something I can't hide from. Before I can spiral further my phone begins to ring. I reach for it blindly not even bothering to check who it is before I answer. I keep my eyes closed and head where it is as I place the phone against my ear.

"Hello?" My voice sounds hollow to my own ears.

"My love." I squeeze my eyes closed tighter, the sound of his voice grating on my frail nerves. "I have been trying to call."

"I was busy." I don't bother trying to be pleasant, Gatson doesn't give a shit about me. He only wants to marry me because of what he will gain.

"Well, I have great news." I only half listen to what he is saying about the wedding and what he would like. I fight the gag that wants to break free when he mentions hosting a masquerade ball the night before the wedding.

"Sure, sounds great," I answer not giving a shit.

"Perfect, Emily will plan everything," he singsongs.

"Oh, the Emily that you fucked in my bathroom?" I couldn't find the strength to hold back that retort. Gatson will make me pay for that when we see each other again but for right now, I just don't care.

"I'll let that slide because I know you are stressed, but I'll make it up to you soon." My phone beeps with another incoming call. I groan.

"Got to go, the dressmaker is calling," I lie then end the call and answer the unknown number.

"Hello?" Now, my tone is laced with annoyance.

"You sound angry." I sit up straighter at the sound of his voice.

"How did you get my number, Bass?" It feels weird saying his name aloud but it's a good weird.

"Hmm, I think I liked it better when you were screaming *beast*." Laughter bubbles out of me. How I can go from feeling like my world is ending minutes ago to laughing shocks me, but I know deep down it's because of the person who is on the other end of this call.

"I'm sure you do. Now what can I do for you? I have a lot of studying to do–"

"How about I be *your* book?" That piques my curiosity.

"How so?"

"Each night, I'll come to you and help you with your studying." I push my lips to the side.

"You really know all this stuff?" I ask, doubting him.

"I know more than you think. I'll tell you what you *need* to know." I mull his words over before an idea strikes.

"And what will this cost me?" The sultry tone of my voice is hard to miss.

"Your body." His simple answer sends a shiver down my spine but I'm not one to take the easy road.

"As tempting as that offer is, I'll pass." I quickly end the call and smile to myself feeling triumphant until I realize who the hell I just baited. "Fuck!" I whisper to the empty room. Something tells me he wouldn't have taken kindly to me hanging up on him. Excitement thrums through me as I think of all the ways he'll make me pay.

Two weeks!

It's been two fucking weeks since I arrived here and eight days since I last saw Bass. I thought he would punish me by taking it out on my body, not fucking ghost me! I asked Mrs. Potts last night where the master was. She says he's out of town and will be back in a few days. For six days I have warred with myself on if I should call him or not. The stubborn half of me keeps me from dialing his number but the other half, the half that misses him when I shouldn't, urges me to call. I've buried myself in studying the history of the families, except, I can't seem to focus in the library now. All I keep thinking about is him fucking me over the very table I am currently sitting at.

"Snap out of it, Bella!" I chastise myself aloud. I roll my shoulders and push all thoughts of my Beast—*my?* Where the hell did that come from? "Focus!" I sit up and continue to read through one of the newer books. I don't know who documents this stuff, but whoever they are, they deserve a pay rise or a medal.

The tension is brewing, Amorro and Vital are fighting but the other families in the city refuse to get involved. If anyone helps one family fight against another they are met with certain death by the elders and that is a fate none of us want. Amorro is pushing in on Vital territory, he is playing a dangerous game. Vital is a good Don, fair and all about the family and making sure everyone inside the families are taken care of.

Amorro is angry because Vital refused to sell his mercenary business. Vital's mercs are like no other. They are a dead shot and leave no evidence behind. All the families come to him to get an enemy taken care of, they are that good. Amorro only wants the merc business so he can feel important. The guy is only about himself which is why I fear for the safety of my friend. He has grown lax since the birth of his second son, who is only a few weeks old. His sons are his sole focus since losing his wife to meningitis after she gave birth.

I lean back in my chair and cross my arms over my chest. I have searched the shelves dozens of times and can't find any more books written after this one. Something isn't adding up. I feel like I am missing a key piece of information but I can't figure out why anybody would want to hide the history of my family from me. There is only one person I can think of who would know the truth and I refuse to give in to him. I would rather fail than call him. I go back to reading the book hoping that it will give me a clue as to what I am missing.

The elders are holding a mandatory sumner, all the heads of their families and their seconds must attend. When a sumner is called, no one knows the location. A driver is sent to collect the two men who are blindfolded and then driven to and from the sumner. Unease can be felt amongst the ranks. Sumners are not something that happens often, in fact the last sumner was called nearly two decades ago when Mikale was elected to serve on the elder council as a founding father when his time came

I gasp, I knew papi was on the elder council but I had no idea how he was chosen to be one of them. I didn't see much of my grandfather growing up but he always calls and facetimes. He and my father don't see eye to eye. Papi nearly had a stroke when I told him that my father used to beat my mother and hurts me. Papi cannot interfere or help me without proof. So many times I wanted to run to him and beg him to help me but my father somehow knew what I wanted to do and would lock me in my room without a way to contact him. Papi is the one who refused my pledge to rid the families of the three month lockout to learn the history of the families. Only girls have to participate in the lockout. Believe it or not, a lot of families marry their daughters off at thirteen to someone they know so they don't have to be used like chattel in a bargain. Not my father though.

The sumner was long, it went on for five days before a decision was reached. Vital won, Amorro was forced to hand over the land he acquired without permission over to Vital. The elders ordered Amorro to stay within his own territory unless Vital gave his okay. The elders tried to broker peace between the two warring families. Vital agreed and so did Amorro but even I could tell this war wasn't over. Amorro isn't the type of man to give up.

It's been a month since the sumner and everything has been quiet. Amorro hasn't tried anything and no one seems to have heard from him. We did receive word from an informant that he was trying to broker peace with the Polish mafia, foolish man. The Polish would fool him into thinking they would help him only to rob him blind and then dispose of his body. They are notorious for that. The elders don't allow any dealings with the Polish because of this. The only way they would change their minds is if there were to be a marriage brokered for peace. Out of the six families, no one has a daughter to marry off to the Polish Don's newborn son.

Holy fuck! I scrub my hands down my face. The polish newborn is Gatson and I'm the first girl to be born into the six families in decades.

We received word that an attack is brewing against the Amorro family. Vital was shocked to receive a call for help from Amorro himself. Vital being the man he is, sent his mercs to guard Amorro and his territory leaving himself wide open for an attack. Amorro was clever, he used Vital's status as the High Don against him. Vital's job is to protect the five families under him. Amorro knew he couldn't refuse and that's when it happened. Amorro and his men raided the Vital family home killing everyone, even Santos, Vital's oldest son and made Vital watch as he did it.

I turn to the last page of the book with tears blurring my vision.

Proof should have been given to the founding fathers but in order to do that, one would have to expose the secret he hid. Without a way to know for sure if Mikale was neutral or not, the decision was made to hide the truth until the time was right. That time will be upon us in mere years, Amorro has no idea what he has started but I can assure you, he will know what he did wrong when the time comes. I pray that the right decision was made to hide this truth.

The life that is lived will ensure war, and vengeance will be claimed by the heir.

I slump back in my chair reeling. There has to be more. This can't be the last book, right? My father orchestrated the murder of an entire family—he even killed children! What kind of man could do such a thing? I feel the bile rise up my throat and swallow numerous times so I don't throw up at the thought of a murderer being my father. Don't get me wrong, I'm not naive enough to think he hasn't killed people but I never thought it was in cold blood. I can't help rereading the last page over and over again, until a thought hits me.

If there aren't any more books, then I need to find the person who wrote these entries, they are handwritten. Surly Mrs. Potts or Father Maurice would know. I have no idea why I am so invested in this but a need burns inside me to find justice for this family, for those children that were taken from this earth well before their time, because of the greed of my own freaking father. I suddenly feel dirty. I grab my phone, laptop and book, then rush from the room. I clutch my belongings to my chest and practically run to my room, needing to shower and scrub the filth I feel clinging to me off my body.

CHAPTER ELEVEN

BEAST

Pulling into the drive of Lumiere, I normally dread the loneliness that ensues the moment I step foot through those front doors but not this time. Being away for over a week wasn't part of the plan but from the moment I landed in Bolivia, shit went south. It took more time than I thought to convince some of them to come back and pledge allegiance to me. I refused to leave until I had the numbers I needed as I will get one shot at this and I can't afford to fuck it up. The driver takes me around the back to the rear entrance. I'm not like those pompous rich dicks who wait for their door to be opened for them, I do that shit myself. I grab my duffle from Dean, he is the only driver I ever use. The guy is on retainer and I mutter my thanks before heading inside. It's late and I'm fucking exhausted but the need to see her propels me to go to her first before I crash for the night.

I drop my duffle outside her door, grip the handle and twist. "The fuck?" I mutter to myself. I attempt to turn the handle again but it's locked. Since when the hell did she start locking her door? I glare at the stupid fucking door for a second before snatching my duffle off the ground and storming toward my wing. I'm pissed as fuck at her for locking me out but stupid girl, I have a master key. The second I step into my room I sigh in contentment. I love being in my own space and not having to wear a mask—each time I travel, I always wear a mask and never allow anyone to see me. I decide to take a quick shower, needing to wash off after a long ass flight. I fucking hate flying. Something about the cabin pressure always makes me feel uneasy and being trapped in a metal box and leaving the fate of my life in a stranger's hands. I wrap a towel around my waist as I step out of the shower, there is no mirror in my bathroom. I had them all removed not wanting to see myself.

I make quick work of changing into some sweats and pull a hoodie over my head not worrying about a shirt. I grab the master key from my side draw before I ready to leave my room, but I grind to a stop in front of the monitor on my desk in here. I lean in close certain that I am seeing things except I'm not. Right there on the screen, I see Bella on a makeshift bed in the library with books scattered all around her. She's moved the bedside lamp from her room in there. What the fuck is she doing? I grit my teeth so fucking hard when I see Chip enter the lenses of the camera carrying a stack of books in his arms. The little fucker drops onto the makeshift bed next to her, he says something and she begins to laugh. Anger thrums through me. I drop into my chair and unmute the audio, needing to know what the fuck they are talking about. If he's laid a single fucking finger on her I'll kill him.

"Seriously, Bella, you stink." I frown, she finds him mocking her odor funny?

"You say the sweetest things, Chippy." The sound of

her voice has a smile tugging at the corners of my mouth. She grabs two books from him before he sets the rest down in front of himself. I recognize those books, she's going back to the beginning. Why?

"You know this is going to take us weeks, right?" Her shoulders slump at his words. I cock my head to the side slightly confused why she seems upset.

"I know. It sounds crazy but I need to find out why my father did what he did. He murdered an entire family Chip and I can't let that go." My eyes snap wide.

"You're nothing like your father, Bella," Chip says as he nudges his shoulder into hers. I clench my hands into fists.

"How can you be so sure? What If I grow up and end up just like him? I couldn't handle that. He needs to pay for what he did, it makes me sick knowing that he killed children. In the book it said he made their father watch." My breath lodges in my throat. "What kind of person could do something like that?" Chip places the book he was holding on the ground and swivels around to face her. He grabs her hands and holds them in his. I dart my gaze between the two of them trying to decipher if something is going on.

"Bella, I promised you that I would help you find the answers you need, which I plan to do, but you need to study as well. I would never forgive myself if something happened to you because you failed this test." I growl at the screen. What the fuck is he doing?! "Just remember what you read, okay? Absorb those words and mull them over until they make sense." What the fuck is he saying?

"Why can't you just tell me?" she begs. I scowl at the screen when Chip smiles at her sadly.

"Unfortunately, I can't. In order for no one to contest this you must be able to answer honestly and explain how you found the answer. Nothing like this has ever happened before and you, Bella, are the last hope for someone."

"Okay. Enough of this, we need to get through these books and find out how Phillipe Amorro managed to become the Don. There has to be something in these books." I sit here for nearly two hours watching them scour the pages of the old diaries. I don't know who made it compulsory for each family to be documented or why girls had to partake in the lockout but I'm not mad about it. Bella is the third girl to ever come here for a lockout. Sadly though, the first two failed and were executed by their own fathers. I refuse to allow Bella to follow in their footsteps. In the last two weeks I have felt a need to step out of the shadows. A fight inside me has been brewing for years but I never had the desire to execute this plan until meeting her.

Another hour passes before they both fall asleep. Chip is face down in his book while she falls asleep leaning against the small table that holds the lamp. I push to my feet and head for the library. I should leave her be, let her go but that is easier said than done when she is living under my roof for another ten weeks. I quietly push the door to the library open and leave it ajar as I make my way to the lamp. I turn the lamp off before I bend down and scoop her into my arms bride style. She snuggles into my chest as I carry her from the room, leaving Chip as he is. Serves the asshole right for trying to encroach on my territory while I was away. He'll be fucking hearing from me the second he awakes. I'm halfway to her room when she slowly blinks her eyes open. I slow my steps expecting her to scream.

"I'm not fucking you," she mumbles sleepily. I snort as I continue walking.

"It's pitch black, how can you even see who I am?" She nuzzles her head against my chest and yawns.

"I know it's you, Beast." Tension drains from me at the fact she does know it's me. I'll admit, I was fucked off thinking she had no idea it was me when she refused to fuck me.

"How?" I ask quietly as I reach the hallway to her room.

"My body betrays me and comes alive whenever you're near," she mumbles into my chest before sleep claims her again. I stop outside her door and fish the key awkwardly out of my pocket. I unlock it and push it open with my back, careful not to hit her head on the door as I enter. I place her in bed and pull the covers over her before drawing her curtains closed—it's close to dawn and I'm ready to pass out. I head for the door but her words stop me dead in my tracks. "I missed you," she mutters. I peer over my shoulder to find her fast asleep, a small smile tugs at my lips.

"I missed you too, Beauty," I whisper before leaving her room.

I've been stuck in my office since eight this morning. I managed to get a couple hours of sleep last night after putting Bella to bed. I don't sleep often, whenever I close my eyes the demons of my past come to haunt me. I rub my tired eyes and take a deep breath just as the door opens to reveal Maurice and Chip. I nod for them to come in. The sight of Chip's smile aggravates me, the little fucker needs to be put in his place and learn that Bella is off limits to him. She is mine!

Mine? Where the fuck did that come from? I push that thought away as they take a seat in the two chairs in front of my desk. I turn away from my Mac and face them, waiting to see what the hell they want.

"How was your trip?" Maurice asks.

"Good," I clip out.

"Someone is grumpy today," Chip teases. I glare at the fucker.

"What the fuck do you want, Chip?" I growl. He doesn't cower under the pressure of my gaze.

"I think Bella needs to get out of here for a bit, maybe go for a hike in the woods or something." I narrow my eyes, a few days with her and now suddenly he knows what she needs?

"He's right, Bass. She is too consumed by these books and isn't absorbing anything because she is on a hunt for answers."

"Answers for what, old man?" I snap. Maurice shoots me a displeased look.

"She wants to find out what happened to the Vital family. She needs to take a break. The girl is clever and she will figure it out if she isn't distracted and call me crazy, but I think you might just be the person to... occupy her?" His innuendo doesn't take a genius to figure out. He wants me to fuck her senseless so she will stop searching for the truth.

"I can take her on a hike and then have her back by supper time?" Chip offers. I cut my cold stare to him.

"When did you two get so close, Chippy?" I mock, his eyes narrow.

"How about not watching us on the camera and just come hang out?" The challenge in his tone grates on my already frayed nerves.

"You forget who runs shit here," I grit out through clenched teeth, the insulant prick rolls his eyes.

"How could I forget? You're the boss who stays hidden

and stalks us on cameras but can't find it within yourself to actually step out of the darkness or from behind a screen to be seen." I'm on my feet within a second glaring down at the fucker Maurice rises to his feet, ready to protect the boy if he needs to. Chip slowly rises to his feet and holds my angry glare with one of his own. "I'm not trying to be a dick, Bass. I can see she actually likes you and she has no fucking idea who you are. For what it's worth, I'm only helping her because *you* won't. She is a fucking cool chick. Maybe you would know that if you took the time to talk to her instead of just making her scream your name for us all to hear."

CHAPTER TWELVE

BELLA

When Chip came to me an hour ago and suggested taking a break and getting outside for a bit, I didn't expect him to take me deep into the woods for some rec time! I hate sports, I hate walking, I don't even walk through a shopping mall, and the closest I get to a mall is online shopping! I love nature but I can love its beauty from a chair on the back deck or something, not walking through it sweating in places no woman should ever sweat.

"Come on, Bella, we're nearly there." I glare at his back.

"You said that an hour ago!" I snap angrily, which just causes him to chuckle. I want to poke his eyes out, I haven't had a good start to the day. Waking up this morning in my own bed gave me a scare until I realized I wasn't dreaming last night. Bass is here and carried me to bed. I was pissed when I didn't find a note or a text saying he was sorry for leaving me on own pretty much. I jumped at the offer to get out of the house with Chip, I thought maybe we were going somewhere fun, not fucking hiking!

We continue up the incline of the hill for another ten minutes. "We're here," Chip sings happily, which just annoys me. How is he not a sweating mess like me? I reach the top and gasp. "Told you it was worth it." Words fail me so I just nod. I can see the whole city from here, the buildings looking small from this distance. Chip points to the left and I follow his pointed finger to see Lumiere below. The old church looks eerie, almost gothic-like from this vantage point. The stained glass windows can just be made out and I see the rose bushes that stand proudly in the distance and that's when a question burns in my mind.

"Why can't anyone touch the roses?" I see him stiffen out of the corner of my eye. I turn to face him but he keeps his gaze focused ahead. The strained look on his face tells me he is debating if he should tell me or not.

"It's the only thing in the world that he finds beautiful." A pang of sadness hits me in the chest. "Bass doesn't view the world as we do. He sees darkness and shadows where we all see colors, beauty, happiness, and even love."

"You make it sound like he has never loved before," I scoff. He turns his head toward me, the solemn look on his face has my eyes widening in surprise. "Holy shit," I breathe out.

"Bass has never loved a single person in his life. Don't get me wrong, he cares about me, Mrs. Potts, and Maurice but he has never allowed himself to get close enough to us to love." My face contorts as pity blooms inside me for the man who hides from the world.

"The roses?" I whisper, he smiles sadly and nods.

"They are the only thing he has ever cared enough about to nurture and care for. They are the closest thing he has ever felt close to love to." I drop my gaze to the ground beneath us, having never heard something so sad in my life.

What a lonely way to live. Love is what makes life worth living. Having your heart broken is painful and sucks but it's what makes living special. to have never loved before must be agony.

"It's better to have loved and lost than to never have loved at all." My whispered words are carried away on the breeze, the anger I felt toward him earlier evaporates instantly.

"It's hard to love when all you have known your whole life is pain and suffering." Chip's gaze bores into mine holding my attention. "Don't let his asshole ways and over-the-top alpha possessive ways scare you off, Bella. We have all seen a change in him since you arrived." I frown.

"Chip, I don't even know him."

He smiles knowingly. "I don't believe that. If you didn't know him you wouldn't be sleeping with him now, would you?" My eyes widen to the size of dinner plates. "Relax, nothing that happens inside Lumiere ever leaves its walls. Your secret is safe." A whoosh of air escapes me.

"We know each other intimately but not emotionally. There is a difference, Chip."

"Is there though?" I frown but he doesn't give me a chance to question him as he leads the way back. I throw my head back and groan.

"I hate you," I mutter under my breath. He laughs and the urge to throw something at the back of his head is fucking strong.

"The faster we get back, the faster you can soak in that tub of yours." I moan at the thought of soaking in the tub until my muscles relax. My pace quickens, wanting to get back as fast as possible. I overtake Chip and his laughter follows me the whole way.

The moment we get back, I race to my room, peel off my sweaty clothes and get in the tub that Mrs. Potts has run for me. The woman is a mind reader and I owe her a huge thanks for the forethought of knowing I would need this. My hair is piled on top of my head, my eyes are closed as I rest back and enjoy this moment. I didn't realize how much I needed to get out of the house and take a break from studying until now. The moment the light vanishes, I smile and slowly open my eyes, the hairs on the nape of my neck stand on end alerting me to his presence. Anticipation thrums through me, my nipples beginning to grow hard at the thought of him and a dull ache begins to form between my thighs.

"As tempting as that sounds, I'll pass." I can't help the laughter that surges out of me hearing him throw the words I said to him on the phone at me. My laughter dies the second he grips my hair and pulls me up until I'm kneeling in the tub. I hate that he never lets me see him in the light. I didn't realize how much time must have passed since I'd been in the tub, I should have known it was night out the moment he appeared. I feel his lips ghost over mine as he speaks, sending a shiver down my spine. "I guess I'll just have to remind you how good I make you feel so you'll change your mind, huh?"

I smile against his lips electing a growl from him. "Do your worst, *Beast*," I taunt. His other hand wraps around my neck so fast I don't have time to prepare. He pulls me to my feet using his grip on my neck and hair. I attempt to get out of the lukewarm water but he yanks my hair back holding me in place. Something must be wrong with me if

I'm getting hot and wet from the way he is manhandling me. I lift my eyes just able to make out his features and a surge of happiness runs through me when I see he isn't wearing his hood. I tentatively reach out slowly and run the tips of my fingers along his scarless cheek. I feel him shudder beneath my touch, which fuels my bravado to continue exploring him. I slowly trail them along his chin and brush the pad of my thumb over his full lips. He nips at the tip of my thumb, drawing a gasp from me. He shakes my hand away and buries his face in the crook of my neck.

"Fuck, you smell so good," he moans. I tilt my head to the side, giving him better access. He licks a trail from the base of my neck all the way up to the shell of my ear, then clamps his teeth down on my lobe pulling a cry from me. He removes his hands from my neck and hair and then cups both my tits, brushing his thumbs over my pebbled nipples. I throw my head back and moan. He replaces one of his hands with his hot mouth. I cry out the second he flicks his tongue over the hardened bud. He switches sides and squeezes my other nipple between his fingers at the same time as he bites down on the other side.

"Fuck!" I cry out as I grip his shoulders through his hoodie to steady myself. He continues to suck and lick my nipple while running his free hand down my body, leaving goosebumps in its wake. He stops right on the top of my pussy. I groan, needing him to quell the ache he has caused at my center. He releases my nipple with a pop and then slowly licks his way up to my mouth where he keeps a sliver of space between us. Our eyes lock as he slowly lowers his hand and slips a single finger through my slick folds, drawing a moan from me. He hisses the moment he feels how soaked I am for him. He slips that finger inside me, forcing a cry from me, then pulls it free and I whimper in protest.

"Is this all for me?" he asks huskily as he holds the finger he just had inside me against my lips.

"Yes," I whisper, brushing my lips against his finger and tasting my own arousal.

"Taste it," he growls, then pushes his finger inside my mouth—a shameless moan comes from me at the taste of myself. "You like that?" he asks as he pulls his finger free.

"Yes." I can hear the need in my own voice and right now, I don't give a shit that I sound like a needy bitch, because I am.

He releases his hold on me and steps back, my eyes widen. "Pity. I would love to fuck you but, my offer wasn't tempting enough, right?" I balk at him. He has to be joking, he can't leave me like this!

"You wouldn't?" I say with as much bravado as I can muster in my needy state.

"Oh, Beauty, I really would." The firm tone of his voice tells me he isn't kidding. I growl and stomp my foot in the tub before I hop out and snag my towel from the ground, wrapping it around my body. His laughter only serves to piss me the fuck off. I shoulder past him hating how his laughter grows in volume, so I decide to have the last laugh.

"Show yourself out, would ya? I have an appointment with my *satisfier pro*." His laughter cuts off immediately. I quickly scurry over to my bed and yank the side draw open to grab my O-inducing friend. The second my fingers wrap around it he yanks it from my hand. "Hey!" I shout, then snap my mouth closed when his hand wraps around my throat in a tight grip. I flinch when the sound of something smashing against the wall sounds out. Oh my God, did he just destroy my vibrator? He gets right in my face, his nose brushing against mine, and for the first time I get a clear view of his blue eyes that are spitting fire at me.

"The only one who gets to make you come is me!" The way he says it with such ownership has me rising to the challenge he set down. I pluck up my courage and wrap my arms around his neck. He stiffens but doesn't tell me off or pull out of my hold, good. I press in closer until my lips ghost over his, loving how his eyes narrow cautiously.

"Then that rule better go both ways, Bass. I'm Italian and we Italian women are known for our temper and jealousy."

"Careful, Beauty, you sound like you're getting attached to someone who isn't your intended." His words are like a bucket of ice water being tipped over me. I attempt to pull free of his hold and tell him to leave but then he smashes his lips against mine. He forces my lips apart with his tongue. The second his tongue collides with mine, all rational sense flees me. My arms lock tight around him as he drops his hold on my neck in order to tear the towel from around me. He runs his fingers down my sides then grips the globes of my ass in his hands and lifts me. I lock my legs around him, something feels different. He's never openly let me touch him before or even got this close to me, he always turns me away from him. Chip's words from earlier play through my mind.

We have all seen a change in him since you arrived.

The second his finger slips through my ass cheeks to press against my asshole I tense and gasp into his mouth. He runs that finger through my ass cheeks again, all the way to my pussy where he pushes it inside me. I break the kiss, cupping his cheeks as I moan and press down harder onto his finger. He drops his head, leans forward and sucks my nipple into his mouth as he continues to finger fuck me at an agonizingly slow pace.

"Oh my God, Bass," I moan, loving the feelings, these sensations he draws out of me, it's like he knows what I need even when I don't. It's so crazy to think I have only known him for a couple of weeks yet here I am entrusting him with my body and allowing him inside me. He slips his finger out of me only to use the same finger to press against my asshole. I gasp when he slowly pushes it inside me, and I tense. He releases my nipple and claims my mouth again forcing me to melt into him and relax, pushing in and out of my ass. I focus on the way he is kissing me to distract myself from the slight sting in my ass. After a moment the pain bleeds way to a feeling I haven't experienced before and I find myself pressing against his finger needing more. He groans into my mouth before yanking his finger out and throwing me onto the bed. I scream in fright. "What the hell?" I shout.

"Lean over the edge of the bed!" The demand in his voice has me obeying without hesitation. I shuffle off the bed and over in front of him. "Place your knees on the edge of the bed." I lift my knees and balance on the edge of the bed as I slowly bend forward so I am literally head down, ass up. He grips the globes of my ass, drawing a small moan from me, from this angle he has the perfect view of my exposed pussy and ass. "You gonna be a dirty girl and take whatever the fuck I give you for punishment?" I scrunch my face in confusion.

"Punishment for what?" I ask. He lands a swift smack to my ass. I lurch forward but he's quick to grip my hips and pull me back into place.

"For denying me what is mine." He runs a finger over my puckered hole. "This ass is mine." He trails his finger down until he is pushing it inside my pussy drawing a sharp cry from me. "This tight little cunt is mine, Bella. The only cock that will ever be inside you is mine." The authority with which he says this has me believing him when I know what he says can never remain true. I am promised to another and even if I detest the man I am to marry, I don't have a way out.

Why can't Bass be my intended?

CHAPTER THIRTEEN

BEAST

Fuck I love the way her pussy clamps down on my finger the second I push it inside her. She can try to fight me all she likes but she even said it herself last night, her body knows me, it responds to my touch, my presence. I fucking love how wet she gets for me, she is so willing to allow me to do whatever I want to her, knowing that I will make her feel just as good as she makes me feel. I push a second finger inside her tight cunt and relish in the cry that tears from her.

"Tell me, Beauty, is this mine?"

"Y-yes."

"Will you ever deny me from having what's mine again?" Another moan tumbles from her when I curl my fingers inside her, hitting that spot she loves.

"God, no," she breathes out. I lower to my knees behind her and slip my fingers out as I grip her ass cheeks and part them—fuck, she smells edible. My mouth waters at the sight of her glistening pussy. I swallow and soak in the sight of her perfect ass and cunt for a second. I lick from her clit all the way to her asshole. "Oh fuck!" she cries out when I push the tip of my tongue inside her ass.

"Your punishment is taking my cock in your ass." A shudder rolls through her, making me smirk. I knew she was a dirty girl from the first moment I touched her. "Tell me you want my cock in your ass."

She groans when I push my tongue inside her pussy and push the pad of my thumb flat against her clit. I continue to swirl my finger around her clit as I speak again. "Say it or I stop and leave you on the edge."

"I want you to fuck my ass, Beast." I press to my feet but pause halfway when she continues on. "Then I want to ride your face until you make me come." I growl my approval. I land a swift smack to her ass, before rubbing it to soothe the sting. She fucking loves it when I spank her.

"You don't call the shots here, Bella. I'll fuck you whenever, wherever and however I want. Do you understand?" I push my pants down, freeing my cock, then grip the base of my cock in my hand and hiss. It's that fucking hard it's almost painful. I run the tip of my dick through her slick folds and tease the entrance of her greedy cunt smiling when the dirty little minx tries to push back and pull me inside her. "Agree to my terms or you don't get my cock."

She growls but when she turns her head to the side to look up at me, I can tell from the look on her face she is too far gone and strung out to deny me. "Fine, I agree you can fuck me all the time, I don't care. Just fuck me now, *please*," she begs. Triumph swells inside me, she has no idea what she has agreed to but she will soon enough. I line my cock up with her entrance and slowly push inside her. I love the sight of my cock disappearing inside her, it's a sight I'll never tire of seeing. We both moan in unison the moment I am balls deep inside her, and a small tremor rolls through her as a sigh of contentment slips past her lips.

I slide almost all the way out then grip her hips in a punishing hold as I slam back inside her. She cries out in pleasure. I do this three more times but stop the second I feel her cunt clamping down on my cock. I pull all the way out and part her ass cheeks then spit, the sight of it slowly trailing down her ass pleases me. I rub the head of my cock in the spit before I slowly push against her virgin hole. She tenses, her breaths become ragged as her nerves begin to build. I run a hand up her back trying to ease some of the tension, I may be a controlling fucker but I would never do anything to hurt her intentionally.

"Just breathe. I promise the pain will be worth it and I'll make you feel so good." She nods against the comforter, closes her eyes and begins to take deep breaths. When I feel her ease up, I slowly push against her ass. I grit my teeth and still as soon as my head breaches her tight wall of muscle—fuck, the need to come is overwhelming. The only sounds that can be heard are our heavy breathing. I push in an inch more and halt when a whimper escapes her. I don't push in any further but I do rock my hips back and forth slowly stretching her to accommodate my size. "Fuck that feels good."

"I-I need more, Bass." I groan and give in to her demands and inch in further, I'm halfway inside her when another whimper slips out of her mouth. A cold sweat begins to bead on my brow, fuck it takes everything inside me not to slam the rest of the way inside her. She pushes up until she is on her hands and knees then slowly arches back so her head is resting against my chest. I move my hands from her waist and cup her tits. She moans. The need to kiss her overcomes me, so I do it, then groan at the taste of her.

She reaches around with one of her arms and hooks it around my neck holding me in place as she slowly pushes down on my cock. When I try to break the kiss she grips the hair on the back of my head and keeps it in place.

I pinch her nipples and love the way she gasps into my mouth. I use that moment to break the kiss and slowly push further inside her. She eases herself down on my cock until I'm fully sheathed inside her ass.

"Fuck," I growl.

"Bass, I feel so... full." I grip the back of her hair and push her forward until she is forced to her hands and knees, then I pull her hair until her head is arched back over her back. I've learned that my little beauty loves it when I pull her hair, and I'm more than happy to oblige. I love the feeling of it wrapped around my hand. I brace my other hand on her lower back as I pull out and then thrust back inside. She screams but it's not from the pain this time. I continue thrusting my hips, loving the sound of skin smacking skin sounding out around the room. I growl my approval when she drops down to her right and uses her left hand to rub her clit. "Keep fucking my ass like that, I'm so close."

"You come when I tell you to!" I grit out. She whimpers.

"Oh God, it feels too good," she moans.

"You like my cock in your ass?"

"Fuck," she screams when I slam inside her so hard she shifts forward on the bed. "Yes, keep fucking my ass hard like that." She removes her hand from her clit and braces herself on both hands. Fuck, she is going to come just from me fucking her asshole, she's fucking perfect.

"I'm gonna come deep inside your ass then I'm going to eat that cunt of mine."

"Yes, fuck me then eat your pussy, *my* Beast." Fuck,

hearing her call me her beast has me nearly tipping over the edge. I roar her name so fucking loud there is no doubt in my mind everyone in the house heard it. Shudders ripple through me as I come in her ass, mentally berating myself for not making her come before I did. I inch out of her slowly. The moment I slip free, she tries to move away so I grip her hips and hold her still.

"Where the fuck are you going?"

She hesitates for a second before she finally answers. "I... thought because you came that..." She lets her sentence trail off, I land a slap on each of her ass cheeks loving the moan that slips free from her.

"I told you I want to eat my pussy, so shut the fuck up and stay right there." I drop to my knees behind her and bury my face in her pussy. She cries out when I suck her clit into my mouth, it takes a minute before I feel her already growing taut with tension as she prepares for her orgasm. I lick from her clit to her entrance and growl against her hole when I taste my own cum. I pull back and watch as it slowly drips from her ass to her pussy. Before it can drip on the bed I rub it all over her pussy with my fingers before I bury my face in her cunt and relish in the taste of my own cum mixed in with the taste of her.

"Oh fuck, oh my that is so fucking hot," she says as she reaches back and grips the back of my head, keeping me in place as she pushes back against my tongue chasing her own release. My cock is already growing hard again with the need to fuck her. "Fuck, Bass, I'm coming," she cries out a second before tremors wrack her body. She slumps forward, breathing hard and twitching from her orgasm. I slide onto the bed behind her, slip one arm under her head and pull her toward me so we are both on our sides, then I grip her leg with my free hand and lift it.

"Put my cock in," I whisper in her ear. She shivers but does as I ask. My hips buck forward on their own accord at the feeling of her hand. She guides my cock to her entrance and moans when she feels the tip inside her. "I need to fuck you hard and fast so rub that fucking clit fast." She shakes her head.

"I can't, it's too much," she pleads. I bite down on the side of her neck and grin when she screams.

"Rub that fucking clit now," I command as I slowly push inside her moaning at the feeling of how well she fits me, like a glove. "Do it or you won't be coming for a month." She whimpers but does as I say. I fuck her so hard my balls keep slapping against the fingers that play with her clit.

"Oh God, Bass," she cries as she stops rubbing her clit. I bite down on her neck again but this time when she screams it's in pleasure. "Do it again and make me come," she yells. Fuck, I love how she can come just from my cock being inside her. She's going to be bruised between her legs tomorrow from the ruthless pace I'm fucking her, and a sick part of me loves that I've marked her. I bite down on her neck but this time I suck her flesh into my mouth. She cries out when her orgasm rips through her. The second her pussy squeezes the life out of my cock I explode inside her, grunting my release against her neck.

CHAPTER FOURTEEN

BELLA

It's been over a month since I arrived here, and the past five weeks have been the best weeks of my life. Every morning I go hiking with Chip. I'm starting not to hate the idea of exercise and then we study until supper time but my favorite time of the day is when it isn't light out, the moment darkness descends my body automatically thrums with anticipation, knowing he'll be coming for me. Every night since Bass came back from wherever he went he comes to me. He doesn't care where I am or who is within earshot, he takes me wherever he likes. I blush when I think of what happened last night. Chip and I decided to have supper in the library. We studied quite late and when I went to the second floor to return the books I had, Bass appeared out of nowhere and slammed me against the shelves. He yanked my pants down and fucked me right there where Chip could have come up at any time and caught him with his cock inside me. I tried to remain quiet but Bass being the beast he is wasn't having it. He made sure Chip knew exactly who—what I was doing.

God, that's not even the worst. Mrs. Potts came to change my bedding last week after I had just gotten out of the shower, so I locked myself in the closet to change, only to be met with darkness, shoved to my knees and a cock rammed down my throat. There is no way she didn't hear me choking on Bass's cock. His need for me is insatiable and I would be lying if I said I didn't hunger for him daily. I love waking the next day and feeling the ghost of him inside me. There is just one problem though. The more time that passes, I find my feelings for him growing and even I know that is a bad thing. He and I can never be more than what we are. How I can be falling for someone I have never seen or even really know baffles me. I mean each night we talk and I feel like I know a part of him but I can also tell there is a whole side of him that he keeps hidden from me.

"Do you wanna know what sucks?" I lift my gaze from another dead-end book and look over to Chip, quirking a brow, urging him to continue. "Seven more weeks and then you'll be gone." The reminder that my time here is limited sours my mood, my shoulders droop and I drop my gaze, suddenly feeling robbed. If I wasn't an Amorro I would be free to live my life as I choose, marry whom I want, and become whomever I want to be. Instead, I will be married to garner peace with a man I don't love—I can't even stand to be near him. I'll be trained how to hide bruises beneath my makeup in case he should lose his temper. I'll also have to turn a blind eye to the number of women he fucks. Oh, and I will also have to give birth to his children. "I'm sorry I didn't mean to upset you."

"It's okay, it's not your fault," I say as I reach over and place my hand atop his, trying to smile.

"You don't want to go back, do you?" He stares at me trying to gauge my thoughts but he doesn't need to try hard, I know the answer is written across my face.

"I don't have a choice," I say quietly. Chip sighs and nods. I withdraw my hand and go back to reading. A part of me just wants to say fuck it and run away, catch a plane, and never come back. If I wasn't such a coward, I would pack what measly possessions I have here with me and run and never look back. Except, I am a coward and petrified of what my father would do to me when he found me because he definitely would find me, there is no doubt about that in my mind.

"I wish there was something I could do," Chip mumbles, both our gazes snap toward the library doors when Mrs. Potts walks in with a sour look on her face that puts me on edge. Mrs. Potts is always smiling and beaming with happiness but right at this minute, she looks like she swallowed a lemon. She stands a couple of feet inside the doorway and clasps her hands in front of her. "What's wrong?" I can hear the note of concern in Chip's voice. She pulls her gaze from my friend to look at me and I frown.

"Deary, could you follow me, please?" I climb to my feet without hesitation. Chip does the same and follows after me as Mrs. Potts leads the way out of the library. I begin to feel nervous as we make our way toward the staircase leading us down to the foyer. I peer at Chip over my shoulder, he shrugs his shoulders telling me he has no idea what is going on either. We descend the stairs and the closer we get to the landing, I notice that Mrs. Potts grows stiff with tension. The moment my feet hit the wooden floor everything inside me ceases, my blood turns to ice and my head begins to spin at the sound of his voice.

"My love!" I'm standing here frozen in shock with Chip

at my back and Gatson rushing to my front. Mrs. Potts steps out of the way at the last second. Gatson grips my shoulders and hurls me into him, I'm too stunned to do anything except stand here and let him hug me. "God, I have missed you," he says in a sickly sweet voice as he puts some space between us but keeps his hands on my shoulders. He leans forward and places a chaste kiss on my lips, and the sharp intake of breath from behind me snaps me out of my stupor. I push against his chest forcing him back. He frowns but says nothing as I sidestep him and take a couple of steps away from the stairs where Chip remains. Gatson looks to Chip, smiles and offers his hand. "Gatson Kaluza," he says proudly. Chip looks from his hand then back to him, quirks a brow, and says,

"Uh-huh." That's all he says before sidestepping Gatson as I did. He stops beside me and places a hand on my shoulder and whispers low enough for only me to hear. "You are safe here. Bass won't let him do anything to you." The reminder of Bass being in this very house where Gatson now stands has me filling with anxiety. Mrs. Potts and Chip exit the foyer heading for the kitchen, leaving me here with Gatson, alone.

He loudly exhales the moment the kitchen door closes and shrugs his shoulders. "He seems like a—"

I cut him off, not wanting to hear what he has to say about my friend. "What are you doing here, Gatson?" He keeps that fake smile on his face as he closes the distance I put between us and cups my face like he has the right to touch me. The feeling of his hands on my skin repulses me. There is no spark or fire brewing in my belly, not like when Bass touches me. All my Beast has to do is enter the room and I'm thrumming with need ready to jump his bones.

"I'm here to see my fiancée, is that a crime?" His voice

may sound light and easy, but the hold he has on my face hardens and I fight the flinch that wants to break free.

"Of course not," I grit out. He smiles approvingly and steps back.

"Now, why don't you show me what you have been studying?" I open my mouth to deny him, not wanting him anywhere near my haven of peace. That is what the library has become for me, it's my sacred place but I'm cut off by Father Maurice.

"The library is off limits to non-staff and visiting personal." Father Maurice glides down the stairs with a miffed look on his weathered face. Gatson steps beside me and wraps an arm around my shoulder pulling me into his side. Father Maurice doesn't miss Gatson's display of possessiveness but he doesn't comment, just places his hands in front of him and smiles politely. "Did you have an appointment?"

"For what?" Gatson sounds annoyed.

"Well, we don't get visitors here and the only people who drop by are here to speak with the master, but by appointment only, of course." Father Maurice sounds friendly but I can tell he is pissed off, Gatson is too self-absorbed to notice the priest is mocking him. He knows exactly who Gatson is but refuses to give him the satisfaction of letting him know this. The grip Gatson has on me tightens. I flinch but try to mask it quickly and the look on the priest's face tells me he saw it, his eyes crinkling at the corners.

"Well, I am neither of those," Gatson says with an edge of cockiness to his voice. "I am merely here to visit my fiancée whom I have missed dearly, so if you would excuse us." He doesn't wait for a reply as he leads me toward the front door, the hairs on the back of my neck stand on end as he opens it. I peer over my shoulder and look up to the second story, my mouth dropping open in shock. Right there in broad daylight with his hood up gripping the banister in a vice-like grip is my Beast, his blue eyes boring into me. I stumble as Gatson pulls me out of the house, I don't remove my gaze from his until the moment Gatson shuts the front door, blocking him from my sight. Anger roars to life inside me that he would dare cut me off seeing my Beast for the first time. I pull free of his hold and put a few feet of space between us.

"What the hell are you doing here?" I seethe. I don't give a shit that I'll pay for my outburst when I return home. All I care about is the fact that my guy is inside that house and I'm stuck out here with this pig of a man, the sight of him disgusts me. He thinks the five o'clock shadow that he sports year round makes him look more appealing but it doesn't. He has his black hair cut weekly and spends an ungodly amount of time styling it every morning. His brown eyes shoot daggers at me as he lifts his upper lip in a snarl. God, you can't even call what he has lips, they look like a duck beak they are that fucking small.

"Philippe sent me to check on your progress," he grits out. "You would be wise to remember who you are speaking to the next time you mouth off." He grips the lapels of his suit jacket and straightens it. I look at Gatson in a whole new light. He is stick thin, with no muscle or definition, just skin and bones. The guy's legs are the size of a chicken's, his nose is the focal point of his face, thanks to its size.

"You can tell my father I am doing what was demanded of me. Now is that all?" I snap angrily. He smiles but it's cold and full of warning as he lazily moves toward me and closes the space between us until his chest is pressed against me, forcing me to crane my head back to see his face. He reaches out and runs his fingers through my hair then grips it and yanks my head back further drawing a hiss of pain from me.

"You'll be cutting this before we leave for Poland." I grind my teeth to try and tamper my anger. I will never cut my hair. "I don't know what it is but something has changed with you. Rest assured, Isabella, I will find out what it is."

"Nothing has changed. I'm still the same prisoner I was five weeks ago." He tugs harder on my hair. I grit my teeth so hard my jaw begins to ache but I refuse to allow a sound to slip free and give him the satisfaction of knowing he is hurting me.

He lowers his face toward mine. I turn away at the last second, refusing to allow him to kiss me. He chuckles but instead of pulling away he runs his nose along my neck. I shudder. He smiles thinking the feeling of him touching me is turning me on when in reality, I shudder from repulsion. He blows his breath inside my ear. I try to pull away but the grip he has on my hair keeps me rooted to the spot.

"I can't wait to fuck the defiance out of you," he whispers in my ear. Bile rises in my throat, forcing me to swallow repeatedly or risk being sick on him. "If you think I will be soft and gentle with you the first time, you're wrong. I'm going to tear you in half with my cock." I slam my eyes closed forcing myself to focus on not throwing up. "Once I have your virgin blood staining my sheets, I'll be sending them to your father so he knows that his daughter is getting fucked like she deserves."

"Do. Your. Worst," I snarl. He nips at the shell of my ear before pulling back and smashing his lips against mine. I try to force him away but he's too strong, so I bite down on his lip hard until I taste blood. He cries out but I still don't release it. The second he slaps me across the face, I release his lip crying out in pain. I nearly fall to the ground until strong arms wrap around me. Before I can register what is happening, I'm shoved behind Chip as he blocks me from Gatson's view.

"You will remove yourself now, boy, this is between me and—"

"You have no jurisdiction here. Isabella is under the care of the Lumiere Church for the next seven weeks." The authority and venom that laces Chip's words shock me, I have never heard my friend sound so... manly. "You are hereby banned from ever entering these grounds again."

"She belongs to me!" Gatson shouts.

"If you don't leave, I will have no choice but to alert the council about your presence here to help your intended cheat on her test." Gatson's sharp intake of breath lets me know Chip has struck a nerve.

"I never helped her, I was merely here to visit—"

Chip cuts him off. "Let's hope the elder council sees it that way. Now, are you leaving or am I calling them?" Gatson growls.

"Once I take over, this place will be the first to go." He tries to peer around Chip to see me but Chip blocks his view of me which I am so grateful for. "Seven weeks, Isabella, and then you are mine!" Chip and I don't move as he storms toward his car. Neither of us makes a move to head inside until his car disappears through the open gates. The second his car disappears from sight is the moment the dam breaks and I burst into tears. Chip spins around and immediately engulfs me in a hug.

CHAPTER FIFTEEN

BEAST

When I saw his car pull into the drive on the cameras in my office I thought nothing of it until I saw him touch her in the foyer. Maurice could sense something was up with me and came round the desk to see for himself. The moment the old man saw what I was looking at, he cursed and rushed from the room.

I watched the entire time and heard everything that was said. My restraint snapped when I saw her flinch in his hold. The motherfucker thought he had the right to touch my girl and then hurt her in my fucking house sealed his death warrant. He's the first to go on my hit list.

The sight of him with his hands on her has me thirsting for his blood to coat my hands and watch the life drain from his eyes. The look of shock on her face at the sight of me had me thinking she was disgusted by the sight but then it hit me, this is her first time ever seeing me in the daylight. She didn't look repulsed or scared at the sight of me. It took every ounce of self-control I possess to not storm down there and tear her away from him and break every fucking bone in his scrawny ass body. The second the door was shut, Chip rushed out of the kitchen and stalked her through the window while I raced back to my office to watch them. Thank fuck I have cameras on the outside and the inside of the house.

When he kissed her, I nearly lost it. But then I saw the fire in her eyes and how she wouldn't succumb to him. I leaned forward, nearly pressing my face against the screen trying to hear what he is saying to her but he's whispering. Then he kisses her again and I see red. I swipe the monitor and everything that is on my desk off.

"Fuck!" I shout, as I tug at my hair, nearly tearing it out. Maurice rushes into my office drawing my attention to him. The look of dread on his face has my stomach sinking. "She left with him?"

He shakes his head. "No, he's gone and she needs you, Bass. Chip had to force him to leave."

"What the fuck did he do?" I say in a voice I don't even recognize.

Maurice takes a breath before he speaks. "He struck her and Chip stepped—" I don't give him a chance to finish before I'm racing out of the room, flying down the stairs and ripping the front open, ready to commit murder but freeze when I see Chip holding her sobbing form. He looks up to me at the sound of my approach. I stand by awkwardly for a second not sure what to do.

"She needs you, Bass," Chip says calmly and nods for me to take her from him. The moment he steps back, I swoop in and scoop her into my arms. She buries her face in the crook of my neck as I walk us back inside. Maurice and Mrs. Potts stand to the side with worried looks on their faces. I keep pushing forward and taking the stairs two at a time heading straight for her room. I kick the door shut behind us and walk us to her bed where I sit on the edge and just hold her against me as she soaks my hoodie with her tears. The urge to take away her pain and suffering consumes me, I want to be the savior she needs me to be but I'm not that guy. I'm the dirty secret she will have to live the rest of her life with. I'm nothing more than a warm body to pass the time with.

"I fucking hate him!" she chokes out. As if my body knows what to do without my mind leading it, my arms band around her tighter as I kiss the top of her head. "I need you to erase his touch," she whimpers, lifts her head and looks up at me. The glassy look in her eyes tells me she isn't even really seeing me right now, she's too lost in her own head to process that she is looking directly at me without the cover of darkness.

"You don't know what you want right now," I rasp out. Her eyes narrow angrily before she shoves me away and nearly falls to the ground, but I grab her before she can hit the floor. She pushes away from me and climbs to her feet seething with anger. I slowly stretch to my full height in front of her. Seeing her this close in the dark is one thing but seeing her in the daylight is a whole different level.

"Fuck you! I fucking hate you," she screams hysterically as tears continue to roll down her cheeks. Words aren't going to get through to her at this moment so I speak through my actions. I snake my arm out, grip the back of her neck and yank her to me. A startled gasp falls from her lips, the glassy look in her eyes disappears the moment I bend low so we are eye to eye. Her eyes suddenly begin to blaze with lust, I press in closer so my lips ghost over hers knowing that it drives her crazy when I do this.

"I almost believed that you hated me for a split second,

until your eyes betrayed you. You can't hate me because I'm buried under your skin, inside your mind, your veins, I'm buried so deep inside you that you have no idea where I begin and you end." Her eyes flick between mine finally seeing clearly, her mouth parts in surprise.

"You're beautiful," she whispers as she slowly reaches up and runs her fingers over the scars that cover my face. My eyes close on their own accord at the feel of her touching my ugly parts. I force myself to stand here and let her explore my face, this is one of the fucking hardest things I have ever done in my life. I have never let anyone see the full extent of the damage that covers my body, but the way she tenderly touches me has hope blooming inside me that she may accept me as I am. "Open your eyes, Bass," she quietly demands. I blink them open slowly, prepared to see a look of disgust or even the lustful look in her eyes to be gone but I see neither of those. She smiles lovingly at me as she cups my cheek and places a soft kiss against my lips. "You don't need to hide from me." My brows draw in.

"Yeah, I do. You have no idea what lays beneath these layers of clothing." I hear the bitterness in my own voice.

"Show me," she urges. I pull free of her hold and drop down on the edge of the bed again. Before I can stop her, she yanks her shirt over her head to reveal a yellow lace bra, then pushes her black yoga pants down her long slender legs revealing a yellow matching thong. The sight has me biting down on my lip. "I started wearing panties, just for you." Fuck this girl is forcing me out of my comfort zone and I'm powerless to fight against her. She walks toward me, and places her hands on the tops of my shoulders before strad dling my lap. My hands instantly grip her ass, drawing a low moan from her.

"What are you doing, Bella?" I grit out when she begins

to pepper kisses along my jaw before making her way to my ear where she sucks my lobe into her mouth, pulling a groan from me.

"Showing you just how beautiful you are." She leans back, grabs one of my hands from her ass and moves it to cup her pussy. Her eyes bore into mine as she says, "Feel how wet I am. Do you see what you do to me? Even without seeing your face your beauty shined through you, like the ways you have touched me, kissed me, and especially in the way you've fucked me. You've shown me just how beautiful you truly are." I hold her gaze as I push her panties to the side and slip a finger through her folds. We both moan in unison. "All you have to do is walk into a room and my panties are instantly destroyed from how wet you make me." The need in her tone is thick. I run my gaze over her face, trying to spot the deceit in her eyes. I see none of that but what I do see is the fucking bruise beginning to take shape on her cheek.

"I'll kill him for touching you," I say with such conviction. Her eyes soften as she runs her fingers through my hair smiling.

"Let's not think about that. I just want to enjoy the time I have here with you." Hearing how resigned she is to her future pisses me off. "Will you let me show you how much you mean to me?" My brows pull in, not understanding what she is saying. When I don't answer, she smiles wide. "Let me take the lead, you just enjoy the ride?" My hesitation must be clear on my face, because she adds, "There is nothing about you I won't love." At the use of the *L* word I stiffen. She uses my stunned state to her advantage, gripping the hem of my hoodie, she lifts it up forcing me to remove my hands from her body. Trepidation wars inside me, the urge to flee and hide in the shadows overwhelms me. "Just keep looking at me, let me be your anchor."

I nod stiffly. As she reaches for the hem of my shirt, my heart begins to pound inside my chest, my breaths turn ragged the second she lifts the shirt. I slowly withdraw my arms and keep them at my side, waiting for her to get her fill then run from the sight of me. Her eyes widen at the sight of me, I keep my face blank of all emotion, I won't allow her to see the hurt on my face when she kicks me out. Except, that isn't what happens. She reaches out and begins to trace the tattoos that cover my arms, neck and chest. Feeling her touch against my bare skin has a shiver rolling down my spine.

"These are beautiful," she whispers before stopping at the tattoo that sits in the center. "What's that?" she asks. I look down at the black rose encased in a glass dome.

"I guess it's like you said, beauty is on the inside, not the outside. This rose represents me being trapped inside myself and this house, its beauty overlooked because it isn't the normal red color. Like me, Bella, I am not normal. I'll never be the guy who is the center of attention or loves being in crowds. I love the solitude I am afforded by living here. No one judges me and I don't have to hide who or what I am."

"Oh, Bass. You had to go back into hiding in your own home because I arrived?" I smile. Reaching up, I run my fingers through her hair loving how the silky strands feel.

"I'm not hiding now," I say quietly. She doesn't use words, she shows me with her body. Leaning down, she presses her lips to mine then slowly pushes me back until I am lying flat on my back. She deepens the kiss as she continues to run her hands all over my naked torso. I've never felt another person's touch on my bare skin like this before. It's strange but also so alluring and I can already tell the feeling of her touching me is going to become an addiction. She breaks our kiss and sits up looking down at me with a sexy smirk, then she shuffles off me only to stand between my legs and reach down to unbutton my jeans. I lift up to help her pull them and my boxers down, my cock slapping against my stomach. I'm rock hard and ready to be buried inside her. "Either suck it or put it inside your cunt. Patience is not one of my virtues, Beauty."

"Uh-uh, you said this was my show so sit back and enjoy the ride, baby." A fire brews in my belly at her words. Weeks ago, she was shy and timid and now I have created a sex demon who loves the thrill of being in control. She reaches behind her back and unclasps her bra, then slips the straps down her arms slowly. I rest up on my elbows enjoying the show she's putting on for me. The lace drops to the floor, she bites down on her lower lip then cups her tits pinching her nipples. "Hmmm," she moans. I grit my teeth and force myself to remain still, refusing to play her game. I know she is trying to force me to break my restraint so she can gloat. My mouth begins to water when she slowly slides her hands down her toned stomach and slips her thumbs into the waistband of her thong. I grip the comforter in a vice-like grip, using all the strength I have inside me to remain where I am and not throw her down on this bed and fuck her, hard.

"Show me my pussy, Beauty." Her eyes are hooded and filled with lust. She slowly pushes her thong down her legs and then holds the scrap of lace out to me. I snatch it off her finger, ball it up and bring it to my nose, inhaling her musky scent. I growl my approval when I feel the wet patch on her panties. I dart my gaze back to her and watch as she slowly works a finger in and out of her pussy, her gaze locked on mine.

"Bass, it feels so good." Her heady tone has my cock twitching.

"If you don't get the fuck on my cock right now, this little game of yours will be over in a second," I grit out through clenched teeth. I am just about to say fuck it to this game of hers when she sticks the finger that was just in her cunt into her mouth and sucks it clean as she climbs on top of me. I ready myself as she straddles my lap, except she doesn't sit on my cock she shuffles up the bed and sits right on my face. I grip her hips and pull her down onto my waiting tongue, her hand gripping my hair and holding me in place as she rocks her hips back and forth, moaning. Right as I feel her begin to tense readying for her impending orgasm she pushes my head against the bed and shifts. I glare up at her. Before I can protest she shimmies down my body, straddles my waist, then grips my cock, lining it up with her entrance before she slowly lowers herself onto me.

"Oh God," she moans out as I watch my cock slowly disappear inside her cunt. The moment I am fully inside her, she cries out, "Fuck, you feel so much deeper this way." I nod, unable to speak thanks to the pleasure radiating through my body. This is a first for me as well. I have always been the one in control, the one on top and fuck me, I feel like a fool for never trying this earlier.

"I need you to move," I grit out. She darts her tongue out to moisten her lips and then nods. She starts off slowly rocking her hips. Once she finds her rhythm and grows in confidence, she places her palms flat on my chest and then begins to bounce up and down on my cock. "Fucking hell, I won't last if you keep doing that," I practically shout.

"Good, because I'm so close and I can't stop it." She

bounces on my cock twice more before she is stilling and screaming my name. I sit up and grip her waist, taking over. I lift her up and down as I thrust my cock into her chasing my own release. She wraps her arms around my neck for something to hold onto as I fuck her like a wild animal. She screams so fucking loud when another orgasm rips through her, and the second her pussy squeezes my cock again I'm done for. I come deep inside her greedy little cunt, marking her as *mine*.

CHAPTER SIXTEEN

BELLA

Bass and I spend the rest of the day in my room. I know it makes him uneasy that I keep staring at him but it's not for the reasons he thinks. He assumes it's because the scars on his face bother me, but that isn't the reason why at all. It's his beauty, he truly has no damn idea how beautiful he is. The man has lashes women pay good money for and don't even get me started on those luscious plump lips—they can rival *Angelina Jolie's*.

When he rolled over earlier and showed me the scars that mark him from the top of his back all the way down to the middle of his thighs, tears ran down my cheeks unchecked. He told me not to cry for him, that his scars are a part of him and they are the reason he never comes out of the darkness. I begged him to tell me the story of who did this to him but he refused. He said the past is called the past for a reason and there is no sense in dwelling on it.

"Stop," he growls but his tone holds no heat. I lay here

with my head propped on his arm, cuddled into his side. Neither of us had the urge to dress, plus, being naked makes it easier for him to slip inside me, his words not mine!

"I'm not doing anything," I defend. He narrows his eyes at me in warning but I can tell he isn't mad, he's just uncomfortable.

"You keep staring and it's... unnerving." His honesty has my heart melting inside me, he's so self-conscious and I hate it.

"Bass, I'm not staring because of the reasons you think." He rolls his eyes not believing a word I'm saying. "I'm staring because I can finally see you. Do you know what it's like to... have a connection with someone but always feel like they are just out of reach?" I don't give him a chance to answer. "I do. You have always been like a figment of my imagination. You're always there but it felt like you were my invisible friend or something." He quirks a brow with a cocky look in his eyes.

"Do all your invisible friends make you come on their cocks?" I gape up at him. "Close your mouth, Bella, or I'll slip my dick inside it." By instinct, I snap my mouth closed and glare at him.

"Are you always thinking about sex?" He shrugs.

"Only when you're around." I huff out my annoyance and get out of bed, ignoring his demand to come back. I slam the bathroom door behind myself before turning the shower on. Before I can even take a step inside the stall, the door is kicked open and a hand clamps down on the back of my neck pushing me forward until I'm smooshed against the cold tiles of the shower stall. I yelp, turning my head to the side. I glare at him over my shoulder, he looks pissed but I don't give a shit. "Don't ever fucking walk away from me again." His tone is firm and filled with warning but I'm too angry to care.

"Fuck you!" I seethe. He smirks and presses in so his front is plastered against my back. I gasp when I feel that he's already hard again. "You are not sticking that thing inside me," I grit out through clenched teeth.

"Whenever. Wherever. However," he says with cocky lilt to his voice. "Anytime I want it, I'll have it. Remember that, Beauty." I fight against his hold, he holds me in place for a second longer before he releases me. I turn around and scowl up at him. The smile on his face only serves to annoy me. Then realization crashes into me, I'm trying to form a deeper bond with him when I shouldn't. We can never be anything more than what we are and that knowledge has me deflating. I'm a stupid girl, here I am mere hours after my intended was just here, standing in a shower with another man, wishing for more when both of us know that can never happen. I close my eyes and try to push the hurt that I'm feeling away and focus on the here and now. I have only just over a month left here before I have to return to my father, pass the test, get married and then move to Poland without getting a say in any of this. The feeling of his hands on my cheeks brings me back to the moment.

"I can't do this," I whisper brokenly. His hands drop from my face immediately. I look up at him with tears obscuring my vision, a look of hurt flashes across his face before he masks it.

"I told you that you wouldn't like the sight of me." His voice is filled with anger and loathing, I shake my head rapidly.

"That's not the reason at all, Bass," I rush to say as I place my hands flat against his chest, imploring him with my gaze to hear the truth in my words. "I can't do this because... I have to marry someone else and I fucking hate it." Tears trail down my cheeks as I admit the truth. "I hate it so much because I have fallen in love with someone I have no business loving." His eyes widen as he inhales sharply. "Marrying Gatson never bothered me before but now, I can't stomach the thought of his hands on me or even having him near me when I know what it feels like to be cherished. You make me feel things I have never felt before, Bass. You have shown me there is more to this life than fulfilling my duty to my family." I sniff and force the last of my words past the lump in my throat. "I love you, but I also hate you for making me feel the way I do. I was able to remain numb and not care about what happens to me but now, all I want is you and I can never fucking have that." Sobs ripped out of me as pain so devastating tears through me.

I stand here breaking apart in front of him and all he does is stand there, no offer of comfort, no hug or whispered words. "I'm sorry, Bella," he says in a tone I have never heard come from him, the look of anguish in his eyes has me crying harder. He cups my face again leaning his forehead against mine. I grip his forearms tightly thinking if I just hold on tight enough nothing will be able to tear us apart. "I should have stayed in the shadows and left you alone. I had no right to take what was never mine but I was powerless to stay away from you." His words have hope sparking to life inside me. "I'll always be watching you from the shadows, Bella. I'll never truly leave you. How can I leave you when you stole the artery that pumps life through my body." I gasp. He smiles and brushes his thumbs under my eyes, wiping away my tears. "You are the rose I never grew but the one I want to nourish most and watch bloom into the beauty that I know you will be." He places a kiss to my forehead before stepping back out of reach. My heart starts to crack knowing that he is about to smash it into a million tiny pieces. "Fight for your life Bella. Fight with everything you have because you deserve more than what you have been given. You deserve more than... *me*."

The moment he turns his back and walks out, I crumble to the floor crying out, the pain that radiates through me is something I have never felt or thought I would ever experience in my life. I cry so fucking loud that my throat begins to grow hoarse. I can barely breathe through the pain, my chest feels like it's caving in. I fell in love with a beast who warned me from the start that he was never obtainable. My stupid ass thought after him revealing himself to me today that he felt the same way I do... He admitted as much without saying those three little words. But still, I wasn't enough for him to stay.

Three weeks later...

I wake, change, eat and study.

Rinse and repeat those tasks daily on autopilot. I don't go hiking with Chip, I barely speak to him or Mrs. Potts anymore. Nothing seems to make me smile. Beast is nowhere to be seen, he doesn't even lurk in the shadows and watch me like he used to. I refuse to call him by any other name now, it hurts too much. Three weeks ago he left me broken and utterly destroyed on the floor of the shower. I managed to cling to my anger for nearly two weeks before that bled way to the pain I constantly feel each and every second of every fucking day. I sit in the library flicking through the books without reading a single word, I'd rather fail this fucking test than marry that arrogant son of bitch and allow him to touch me.

I've been trying to formulate a plan. I have no choice now. I have to come up with a way to get my freedom. I won't let them hurt me anymore, I can't. I can't even confide in Chip for help because I know where his loyalty lies, he can never know about this. No matter how much I wish things were different, they aren't and I need to grow the hell up and remember that before I run out of time. My phone begins to vibrate on the table beside me. I groan knowing that I may be able to ignore Gatson's calls and texts but I can't ignore my fathers. I take a deep breath before I answer the call and place it on speaker as I continue to flick through the book.

"Father," I answer in lieu of a greeting.

"What the fuck do you think you are playing at here, Isabella?" Before I would be worried about his tone and scared of what he might do but now, I'm just pissed off.

"I have no idea what you mean." His sharp intake of air alerts me to the fact my response has shocked him.

His tone is quiet but filled with warning. "Don't think because you are not within my reach that you can speak to me like that. You will return to me in a matter of weeks." The reminder of only having four weeks left here grinds on my nerves. "Why the fuck are you ignoring Gatson?" I roll my eyes, of course, he went crying to my father like a bitch so I decide to lie to him not caring about the consequences.

"Gatson came to visit me—"

He cuts me off before I can finish. "What? When?"

"A couple of weeks ago, he said he missed me."

"What did you do?" he growls.

It makes me sick to say this aloud but I know it's the

only way for him to stay out of this and allow me to continue to ignore Gatson. "He told me he loves that I appear unobtainable, so I thought me ignoring and building the suspense between us would make him seeing me again more... *pleasurable* for him." I fight back the bile that rises in my throat.

My father chuckles darkly. "There may just be help for you after all. Good thinking. Treat em' mean and keep em' keen, aye?" He laughs and it makes me sick.

"Yeah," I say with fake enthusiasm.

"Make sure you make him happy the moment you return, Isabella. I'll deal with Gatson." He doesn't say anything else before he ends the call. I cover my face with hands and fight back the tears threatening to spill. How has my life become such a cluster fuck? Only I would admit to someone for the first time in my life that I love them and they bail on me. I guess my father is right, I'm just not worth anything unless my legs are open.

"Your dad's a dick." I drop my hands and look up to see Chip standing at the other end of the table with a sad smile on his face. I try to muster the strength to return it but I just can't. "You look like shit." I snort out a laugh, he isn't wrong. I hardly shower because being in that stall triggers me. I'm pretty sure I've been wearing the same clothes for at least three days and I can't even remember the last time I washed my hair.

"I have no one to impress. I already have a fiancé waiting for me, so there is that." I can hear the bitterness in my own voice. Chip being the amazing friend that he is doesn't call me on my bitchy attitude, he just nods.

"Well, you look like shit and smell—badly and I have the perfect cure for that." I frown as I smash my lips to the side, annoyed he called me out on my... scent. "Come on, it's not like you're actually reading anyway." I narrow my eyes which just causes him to laugh. He isn't wrong, so I decide to throw caution to the wind and follow him out of the library, not sure exactly where he is taking me. My curiosity peaks when we pass the west wing, dark wooden doors stand proudly at the end of its little hallway. What's in there? "Come on!" I shake my head and continue on. Chip leads me down a hallway I have never been down before, stops at the last door on the right and pushes it open. I follow after him and freeze in the entryway.

"Oh my God," I breath out. Chip smiles and continues further into the room. I don't know how to explain it. It's like something out of a movie—trees, plants and grass line the floors, walls and reach all the way to the roof that isn't a roof, it's glass. Well, a dome really, it reminds of something you would see in an auditorium. In the center is a... rock pool with steam billowing off the top of the water. "What is this place?" I whisper.

"Mrs. Potts loves nature but due to her bad knees she can't walk far. She has always said when she was a child her and her sister would try to find moon pools in the woods." He chuckles fondly. "So Bass decided to make her wish come true and made this place for her." Hearing his name feels like I've been punched in the stomach. I try to keep the pain from my face but Chip sees it. I love him even more for not calling me on it. "So, go change into your bathing suit and come relax with me. Don't say no because I would hate to have to drag you out back and hose you off."

I glare at him. "You wouldn't dare." He pops a brow at me.

"Try me, the choice is yours." I huff and stomp my foot.

"Fine, I'll be back but I'm not doing this because of you, I'm doing it because I want to."

"Hmm, whatever you say," he teases as I march out of the room and head to my room to change, feeling a tiny bit excited to soak in that beautiful pool with my friend. I hate that I think of him and imagine us both relaxing in that pool at night, looking up at the night sky.

CHAPTER SEVENTEEN

BEAST

I thought me lurking in the shadows and following her every move when she first arrived here was bad. I was fucking wrong!

I watch her on the screen of my computer every fucking day. I now have a camera installed in her room, bathroom and closet that she doesn't know about. I even watch her on my phone in bed every night. I love watching her sleep, nah, I just love looking at her. Three weeks have passed and I still crave her like a junkie craves heroin. Walking out on her and hearing her cries or the way she screamed my name begging me to stay shattered the iceberg that encompassed my heart. Now, the artery beats for her and only her. It fucking dumbfounds me how eight weeks ago I couldn't stand the thought of her coming into my home. I tried every-thing to overturn Maurice's decision but it was too late and now, the thought of her leaving here in four weeks without *me,* has me on the verge of laying waste to the fucking world.

I narrow my eyes at the screen, ignoring Maurice as he harps on about the merc's arrival and the plan as I watch her race into her room. I switch to the cameras inside there, she goes straight to her closet and strips naked. My cock leaps to attention at the perfection that is Isabella Amorro. My whole body begins to tingle with the need to touch her. She grabs something from the shelf and to my utter horror I watch as she dresses in a yellow two-piece bathing suit. When she bends over to grab something, I leap out of my chair—the bottoms are a fucking G-string! Maurice snaps his mouth closed as I storm toward the door. The old bastard moves fast and blocks my way.

"Get the fuck out of the way!" I snarl.

"Bass, leave the girl be. Unless you plan to claim your right, you can never have her." I'm breathing so fucking fast my head begins to swim.

"Fuck!" I roar as I turn and slam my fist through the wall, unable to tamper the rage inside me, I do it again but this time my knuckles split.

"Stop!" I turn my head to the side to see Maurice looking at me with a look I have never seen before. "You have hidden away your whole life, Bass. She brought you out of that darkness, take your rightful place and claim Bella as yours. Give her the books and let her choose *you*." I run my hand through my hair and tense when I realize I'm not wearing my hood up. I frown as his words play on repeat in my mind. I stand here in nothing more than a shirt and jeans. I've never not worn a hoodie in... I don't even know how long. Is he right?

I shake my head. "I can't, old man. If I do that there will never be peace for me again. No more shadows just... light." A sad look washes over his face as he reaches out and places a hand on my shoulder.

"Son, the way I see it, that girl blew up your favorite hiding spot and filled it with light. I see it in your eyes, Bass. You love her and I bloody well know she loves you too. That girl has been a mess for weeks now since you walked away from her."

"I can't, Maurice. She has no fucking idea who I really am."

"She doesn't need to, son. She fell in love with this side of you, even when you pushed her away, refused to come into the light, she never let you go. Knowing who you really are won't make her love you more than she already does. If you can stand here and look me in the eyes and tell me you would be okay watching her stand by Gatson's side as he takes everything away from you, then I'll never say another word on this matter again. But, if you can't stand the thought of another man's hands on her, or the thought of her loving someone who isn't you, then you need to change the game plan and leave her be until you claim what is yours, including Bella."

He stands there for a minute, giving me time to think. When I say nothing, he pats my shoulder, smiles and tells me he'll make some calls, before walking out. I shake my head and rush back to my desk and flick through the cameras until I find her in the moon pool with fucking Chip. I'm going to break the little fuckers nose for this stunt. He knew what he was doing, he was the asshole who set up the cameras in her room for me. I enlarge the little box and click it off mute as I recline back in my seat and watch her. The brightness in her eyes has dimmed, the smile she would sport constantly is gone. She looks defeated.

"I know it's a stupid question but, how are you doing?" Chip asks, her shoulders slipping lower beneath the water, she keeps her gaze focused up on the sky as she answers.

"Just peachy. I have four weeks of freedom left before I go home and marry the man of my dreams and let him violate my body every night until he can plant an heir inside me. I can barely contain my excitement, I might even start packing tonight in anticipation of leaving." The sarcasm is thick in her tone, but hearing those fucking words come out of her mouth has a bloodlust pounding inside me. I'll kill that fucker before he ever touches her.

"I wish I could help, Bella–"

"It's not your fault, Chip, none of this is your fault. I'm just angry because..." She cuts herself off and closes her eyes trying to fight back her tears. I reach out and run a single finger over her face, smiling.

Oh, Beauty, you're mine and I'll make it known to the fucking world.

"For what it's worth, Bella, I really do believe Bass cares about you." I tense in my chair.

"If he cared he wouldn't have left me on the shower floor after I just told him I loved him and didn't know how I could leave him behind." Chip's mouth drops open in shock.

"You love him?" She opens her eyes and slowly lulls her head to the side to look at him. I slam my own eyes closed when I see the tears trek down her cheeks, knowing I'm the reason for her pain.

"I wish I didn't." I open my eyes and wait with bated breath for her to continue. "I hate him so much for making me love him, Chip," she sobs, Chip closes the space between them and wraps his arms around her. he clings to him as she falls apart in his arms. I want to go to her, rip her from his arms and hold her but I can't, not yet. I fish my phone from my pocket and dial Maurice's number. He answers on the second ring.

"Bass?"

"Book me a flight, you're coming with me."

"You're going to do it?" The pride that I hear in his tone makes me feel slightly better about this choice.

"This will change everything, Maurice!" I growl.

"Would you rather both of your hearts pay the price for your solitude?" I sigh.

"If it was just mine the answer would be simple."

"True love only happens once in a lifetime, son. The sacrifice you are about to make is nothing compared to the reward you will receive. Everything you have endured up until this moment will be worth it because of *her*."

"I know. Make the arrangements. She can never know until it's time. If they find out, they will kill her. We go ahead with everything as normal, until the time is right."

"She'll have to return to them, Bass." I slam my eyes closed knowing he is right, but in order for this to be official, everything has to be planned meticulously and done right or we'll all be dead.

"I know. She's fucking strong, Maurice. She needs to be kept in the dark, her ignorance to all of this will be what sells it to the elders."

Later that night, I sit on the window ledge in my room staring out at the night sky feeling...freed. After my call with Maurice today, a sense of rightfulness settled over me. I never would have thought I would ever accept the idea of coming out of my shadows to claim what is mine but now, because of a beautiful girl that burst into my life and gave me no choice but to see her, I'm giving up the one thing I swore I never would. A knock sounds at my door. I take a deep breath, I know who it is and I just fucking hope she doesn't confirm what I already suspect.

"Come in." Mrs. Potts appears a second later with a worn look on her face, my shoulders slump. "I'm right, aren't I?" Her eyes meet mine, I can see she is worried about how I'll react to this news.

"I suspect so, yes. Only time will tell for sure though."

I nod. "Am I the only one who didn't know?" Her face falls but she doesn't lie.

"I believe she knew, yes. Chip and Maurice have no idea. I didn't either until you asked me earlier. I would never lie to you, Bass." I smile my thanks. "May I say something?"

"Sure," I breathe out as I lean my head against the glass and stare out at the nighttime sky that is filled with stars.

"I'm so proud of you." Her words have me snapping my head toward her and frowning, certain I heard her wrong.

"What?"

She smiles brightly, her eyes fill with unshed tears. "Twenty-eight years ago when you were brought here, I fell in love with you instantly. You were the most beautiful baby I had ever seen. I could tell you would always be special." I'm stunned silent, she has never spoken to me like this before. "I hate myself for not knowing what Cogsworth was doing to you." She spits his name out like it burns her tongue. "God strike me down, but the day he died was one of the happiest days of my life, I will never admit this again but I pissed on his corpse before it was removed." My brows jump to my hairline, staring at Mrs. Potts like she is a foreign being. "You retreated so far inside yourself after that, I feared you would never step into the light again. You shut yourself off from the world, from all of us and I thought

that you would never experience the joyous feeling of love."
She walks toward me and smiles as she reaches out slowly
with shaky hands to cup my face. A small sob breaks free.

"I never—"

She cuts me off. "Hush now, boy. I raised you better
than to cut a lady off when she is speaking." I bite down on
my tongue to keep from lashing out at her. "See, you really
want to cuss me out and tell me I don't know anything but
you won't. This is also the first time you have let me touch
you since you were eight and that is all thanks to love, my
dear boy. Don't punish her. She is hiding away because she
is frightened, not because of you but *for* you."

"Why?"

"Because she loves you enough to never burden you
with this. She is strong and will do what any women in her
position would do."

I frown but ask, "And what is that?"

"Survive, my dear boy."

"I respect what you are saying but–" Her face falls.
"She will be punished for this, then I'll make it up to her."

CHAPTER EIGHTEEN

BELLA

With just over two weeks left before I have to leave, my mood sours worse each day I wake. I'm ashamed to say I have crept through the house at night, hoping to feel the hairs on the back of my neck stand on end, but it's like he's not even here. I just want to see him one last time before I leave but something inside me knows I will never get to see him again, just like he wants. I've given up on studying. I have no urge to waste what little freedom I have left on learning about bullshit from years ago. The only books I want to read are the ones that hold the history of the Vital family that was murdered by the hands of my disgusting father.

I can't even manage to stomach the thought of food, much less actually eat it. Mrs. Potts has been harping on about me needing to keep up my strength, blah blah blah. I don't care. Her and Maurice have steered clear of me for the last month. I know they know what happened between me and... *him* but neither of them say a thing. Chip is my only constant. On days when I don't want to leave my room, he'll come by and we'll lay in bed all day watching movies on my laptop. He never pushes me to talk, it's almost like he can understand how I feel. On the outside, I look fine, like normal but on the inside, I'm so fucking broken, everything inside me aches, my heart only beats because it has to. I hardly sleep. Every time I close my eyes all I see is his face. I had one day to look upon it before he ripped it away from me. Part of me wonders if it would be easier to let him go if I didn't know what he looked like. You can't miss what you haven't seen, right?

"Stop it!" I say out loud to my dark room, it's after midnight and I still can't sleep. It's this fucking room, every-thing in here reminds me of him—the way he made me feel, how he held me after Gatson left. He helped me realize my own worth without even really trying. He saw *me*, not the heiress or a ticket to the top, he just saw Isabella Amorro. I need to get out of here. I practically leap out of the bed, snag my robe from the floor and decide to head to the moon pool. I love that room, the sky seems so bright and vibrant in there. I make sure to keep quiet not wanting to wake anyone.

When I first got here, the old church creeped me out, but now, I find beauty within its darkness. Just as I near the west wing I slam to a stop and hide behind the wall. I have no idea why I hide but something tells me that I don't want to be seen right now. The hairs on the back of my neck stand up, a shiver treks its way slowly down my spine.

He's here!

"Why can't you just be honest with her!" I stifle my gasp at the sound of Chip's voice, he sounds angry.

"Don't fucking question me." The sound of his voice has my heart rate spiking and my body swaying unsteadily.

"She doesn't need to read the fucking books, don't push me!" God, the grit in his voice really does make him sound like a beast.

"The Vital history is important for her to understand how her father became the head, she will never pass that test without them!" Chip pushes. I strain my hearing at the mention of those books, everyone in this freaking house told me they don't exist! I feel betrayed by Chip, he knew this whole time that there were other books. He helped me search the library and sat with me the whole time as I wracked my brain trying to come up with a reason why they would never continue writing these books.

"She doesn't need to pass, keep her the fuck away from this wing while I'm gone. She hasn't ventured this way until you showed her the fucking moon room. Keep her away for another two weeks and then you're free to go back to whatever the fuck you were doing before her! I leave in the morning and I'm gone for four fucking days. Maurice won't be here, Chip, so don't fuck up!" The way he speaks about me has tears building, he sounds callous and cold. When I hear footsteps I quickly and quietly race back to my room not wanting to be caught eavesdropping.

I slept maybe an hour or two at most, it's not even five in the morning and I've showered, changed into fresh clothes and even brushed my hair and made the bed. I sit on the edge and practically twiddle my thumbs. I concocted a plan that will no doubt go to shit but with Maurice and him out of the house, I only have to worry about Mrs. Potts and Chip, both of whom are normally in bed by eight each night. The sound of tires crunching over gravel draws my attention. Slowly I climb to my feet and move toward the balcony doors, moving the net curtain just enough to see through. The driver climbs out of his car and moves to the back door, opening it. My breath lodges in my throat the moment he comes into view. Black jeans, Chuck Taylors and his signature bloody hoodie with the hood up.

I can't see his face. I know that's probably a good thing but God, I wish I could just see it one last time. He pauses at the open door and hands his duffle bag to the driver who smiles and says something that has him nodding his head. Just as he crouches to get in the car, the hope I had of seeing him again dissipates, until he freezes halfway inside the car and turns back to look up. My breath freezes in my throat as my eyes feast upon his face. It feels like I stare at him for minutes but in truth, it's mere seconds before he tears his gaze from mine and slides inside the car. Call me crazy but the moment the driver closes that door, I feel like a part of my heart was closed in there with him. I watch as Maurice rushes out of the house and heads to the other side of the car. I smile at his flustered state, the poor guy looks stressed and they haven't even left yet.

I wait until the car leaves the gates. The airport is roughly an hour and twenty from here. I used the GPS on my phone to check. I estimate it will take them an hour to clear customs, forty minutes or so before they board, so I have about three hours to kill before they are in the air. That's when I'll make my move, at least that way if there are cameras in that wing, he won't be able to turn around and come back.

I eat breakfast with Chip this morning just so I can gauge where he and Mrs. Potts will be for the day. I ask Chip about Maurice's whereabouts and he lies right to my face telling me he's in the office with Bass. I play my part, smile and nod, then ask what his plans are. He tells me he plans to go for a hike. I decline his offer to accompany him. Mrs. Potts says she will be in the kitchen baking most of the day. With that information I smile my thanks, excuse myself and head upstairs at the same moment Chip slips out the door to go for his hike. Rather than turn right to head to my room, I dart left and rush toward the west wing. I pause at the end of the hallway, staring at the giant wooden doors. Before I can talk myself out of it, I put one leg in front of the other until I'm standing directly in front of them. I reach out and grip the handle, take a deep breath, then twist the knob—it's locked!

"You might be needing this." I scream, spin around and lose my footing, dropping to my ass. My heart beats so fucking fast I swear it will leap out of my chest. Mrs. Potts stands at the end of the tiny hallway holding a key out toward me. I climb to my feet but don't close the space between us.

I eye her warily as I ask, "How did you know I was here?"

The old lady just smiles knowingly at me. Unease begins to creep down my spine. "Deary, I may be old but I am neither blind, deaf or dumb. I have eyes and ears all through this place. I don't need those fancy cameras like my boy does."

"I-I... I was just, I got lost?" I cringe at the sound of my own pathetic lie.

"Bella, if I didn't think you were good for my boy and that your intentions were anything but pure, I would never have disabled the cameras in this house the moment they left and snagged the spare key from his desk." I stare at her in utter disbelief.

"Why?" I whisper, utterly stunned that she is willing to help me. She moves toward me slowly and stops a foot away. She reaches for my hand and places the key inside before curling my fingers over it.

"Because you need the truth of how everyone came to be here, how *he* came to be here. All I ask is that when you learn the truth, you keep an open mind and understand that he didn't have a choice in any of this. He would change the outcome of your fate if he could except, you are the only one with that power."

"What do you mean?" She releases my hand and cups my cheek with a warm smile on her face.

"Read my dear, all you need to know is in those books but don't waste time. He'll realize soon enough that the cameras are down and Chip will not deceive him." She releases me and walks away without another word. Mrs. Potts is full of secrets. I thought I was cunning and smart with my careful planning but obviously not as careful as I thought. It takes me a full minute to snap out of my stupor, then I'm turning around and slipping the key into the hole to unlock the door. I twist the handle and push the heavy door open, then taking a single step inside the room, I pause. My eyes dart around the room, my hand coming up to cover my mouth as I realize this wing isn't an office or a vacant space as I thought, it's *his* room.

The walls are all painted black, the curtains are black, the four poster bed and even the bedding is black. Not a speck of color can be seen in this room. My heart hurts for him. He really meant it when he said that he lives in the shadows. He has a small desk pushed up against the wall with a computer atop it. I walk into the bathroom, and low and behold, everything is black, down to the taps on the sink but it's the vacant spot above the sink that steals my breath

—there is no mirror. I walk into the closet and frown, aside from black only dark blue and white shirts can be seen. All his shoes are bloody black. My eyes are drawn to a lone mirror on the wall. It's beautiful and clearly an antique but what has me stumped is why have one in here but not the bathroom?

I don't waste time pondering that thought as I head back into the bedroom and move to the side of the bed without the desk where I see a stack of books. These ones look newer than the ones in the library but they are still clearly decades old. I run my finger along the spines and a sense of dread washes over me, I just know that whatever these books hold inside them will change everything. He wouldn't have hidden them if they didn't hold a great deal of information inside. I grab the three top ones that are dated the oldest on the spines and climb onto the bed, opening the first book.

Their blood was everywhere, strewn across the walls, carpet, portraits, blinds—it was a sight out of a horror movie. I should have been here! It was my job to protect the Don and the heirs. I found him, alive and unharmed when I arrived at the Vital family estate. I came back to tell the Don that Amarro wasn't even at the estate we were tasked with guarding, and arriving here I now knew why the estate was empty. It was a decoy to get rid of the guards so he could overthrow the head of the *family and take the heirs, except he missed one!*

I gasp. One of the Vital boys lived! This means, if I find the son he can claim his rightful spot as the head of the family and I won't have to go through with this sham of a wedding.

Knowing that there would be a manhunt for the missing child, I had no choice but to hide him, allow him to be raised by another until he comes of age to reclaim what was rightfully his. If I could raise him and keep him with me, I would. I can't because they will be hunting me. I'll return in ten years when some of the heat has dissipated.

I turn the page but that's the last entry in the book, I grab the next one and open it.

It's been a long time since I have written in one of these, almost ten years ago I wrote my last entry. He's ten now which means it's time for me to head back and teach him everything there is to know about who he is. I left him letters hoping that Cogsworth would give them to him when he thought he was ready. Lumiere was the safest place to leave him, knowing that

Amorro would never think to search for him there.

What the hell have I done?

The boy is beaten, and scared and his body is disfigured.

Cogsworth betrayed me when I trusted him!

He read the letters I had left for the boy and chose to dole out punishment on him daily, all because his father had refused to allow him to train the next generation of leaders. Vital believed that all heirs should be taught by their fathers not sent away to be trained by a priest.

I've been here at Lumiere for weeks and still the boy won't come near me or much less speak to me. He obeys Cogsworth like a dog, I threatened to have Cogsworth banished, but he countered and threatened to tell Amorro about the boy. My hands are tied, I can't even tell the boy the truth.

The boy is nearly eighteen now. He and I have built a relationship of sorts. Tonight, I witnessed the extent of Cogsworth's rage. He had the boy on his knees as he whipped him with a Roman scourge. The boy's back is torn to shreds, his backside and legs are marred with scars. I beat Cogsworth, then I used his own weapon against him for ever thinking he could harm the child. He tried to flee Lumiere but I wouldn't allow it. The boy fought for Cogsworth, he was so frightened of him that he would dare to fight me so Cogsworth wouldn't punish him for me stepping out of line. I need to find a way to get him to see that he owns Lumiere. That Cogsworth works for him. I just need him to hear me out.

CHAPTER NINETEEN

BELLA

Ten years ago...

The rain pelts down on the glass windows of Lumiere. Cogsworth, Mrs. Potts, myself, the boy and Chip all sit around the table. Something is off, the boy is tense and glaring across the table at Cogsworth. The fat bastard sits there eating like he didn't just spend an hour whipping the boy because he made a noise as he passed the priest's office. Priest or not, I plan to end his miserable life tonight. I will not watch the boy go through this any longer.

I managed to corner Cogsworth after

supper. I demanded he returns the letters along with the birth certificate. He laughed and refused, telling me if I tried to interfere again he would call Amorro himself and deliver the boy to him. I've wanted to kill Cogsworth for years now, but taking him out means drawing attention to Lumiere and I cannot take that risk. If he were to meet his end someone would need to take over, and that person can never be me. Even after all these years the older generation would recognize me and know I was Vital's second and most trusted Capo.

As the bell tolled midnight the sounds of screams could be heard. I raced from my room to a sight so ungodly I had to fight back the bile that threatened to break free. The body isn't huddled in the corner, using the shadows to conceal himself from view. He stands there shirtless, staring down at Cogsworth's body, which is sliced open from the shards of glass from the broken mirror. That's when I see the letters strewn across the wooden floor of the office. He found them!

The boy agreed to take over. Mrs. Potts, Chip, myself and the boy agreed to never mention this night again. We disposed of the body, and cleaned up the mess—this night would never be mentioned again. This is a secret we would take to our graves. I asked the boy what happened, he said after he was beaten earlier, he was tasked with cleaning the office. He broke the mirror accidentally and then the letters tumbled out from behind the glass. He read them all. At dinner, he told me his mind was made up that Cogsworth would not survive the night.

I write this for all to know, Lumiere is not the place of solace you are all led to believe, the lockout is an age old tradition. Cogsworth never allowed the girls to learn the key answers to pass the test, I am here to tell each of you young ladies if you are reading this that you have a choice.

'If the intended shall fail to marry their chosen, the heir to the prior Don will be accepted as replacement The intended must decree in front of the old families, the new, their intended and the prior heir.'

'The intended may never be swayed by the previous heir, all must be the choice of the intended. The heir may never reveal who they are or which family they belong to. From the moment of the lockout, the clock will start, allowing the intended three months to change their mind.'

You are never to speak a word of what you just read, dig through the archives, find the family trees of every Don, you are able to pick someone from any line as long as they are a blood relative. The moment you announce this, your marriage to your intended with be nullified and you will be given twelve months to find your heir.

This is the last entry you will read from me, the heir has taken over this task, wanting to document his life and tell you his story of pain, struggle and how he became the beast of this old church. Here at Lumière, things go bump in the night, the shadows hide the danger that lurks around every corner.

He thinks he is ruined, damaged and unlovable. He is the true heir and if you are strong enough to have lasted the three months of the lockout, then you might just be worthy. If *you are smart enough to figure out who he is, and where he truly belongs, then maybe, just maybe you may be worthy of him.*

I offered to go to the council with the proof, now that he was of age. He refused. We couldn't be sure that the council hadn't been bought by Amorro. We have a plan and one day, when he is ready, he will come for his throne.

This Capo has now taken on the role of father. These entries will mean nothing to you unless you know the past. Dig through the others, follow the trail and I give you my word that the answer is hidden in the shadows of this very church.

"Holy shit!" I snap the book closed and place it back where I found it before racing from the room. I run, not stopping until I reach my own room. I slam the door closed and lock it before grabbing my phone off the bedside table. I scroll through my contacts, my finger hovering above his number, not sure he'll even answer. Before I can talk myself out of it, I hit dial and chew on my thumbnail as I wait nervously for him to answer. I'm about to hang up when he finally answers.

"Isabella, what a surprise." A whoosh of air escapes me at the sound of his voice.

"I'm sorry to call but I need your help, please. I wouldn't be asking if this wasn't a matter of life and death."

"Where are you?" He sounds on edge now.

"Lumiere," I whisper afraid he'll say no.

"You found the answer didn't you?" My eyes widen.

"Y-you knew?" I hear the smile in his voice as he speaks.

"I always knew you were smart. I'll have a car there within the hour, he'll bring you straight to me." Tears of gratefulness cloud my vision.

"Thank you." I can hear how watery my own voice sounds.

"I love you, sweet girl."

I smile. "I love you too."

I pack all my things and carry them quietly down the stairs when I get a text telling me the car is at the gates. Just as I reach the foyer Mrs. Potts and Chip come into view. She looks sad but happy, Chip has a look of betrayal across his face. He has no idea what I was doing this morning and no doubt thinks I'm running back to Gatson. I can't tell him differently. I need them all to remain in the dark. If this plan falls through, I don't want any of them implicated. I drop my bags by the door and look at each of them. I hate I'm leaving but there is a small chance that I can make this happen, I need to take it.

"Thank you both for... everything." Mrs. Potts smiles and Chip just snorts, clearly pissed off at me.

"You, my dear, are a breath of fresh air," she says as she comes to me and engulfs me in a hug. I'm woman enough to admit tears sting the backs of my eyes. "I hope you succeed," she whispers in my ear.

"Me too," I say as we pull apart. Chip moves to me but keeps a small distance between us.

"He just needs time–"

I cut Chip off. "I know. I can't wait any longer. I have to do this but I swear none of this is what you think." He nods but I can see the regret in his gaze. He says nothing as he turns and walks away without a goodbye, and my shoulders slump.

"When the time comes or if it doesn't, I will tell them both about how brave you were to even try and do this."

"If... if this doesn't work can you please tell him–"

"No, dear, you tell him. He won't allow you to leave him. That boy can be hard-headed and take longer than a turtle to get his head right, but when he does, be ready because he will come for you full force and destroy anything that tries to keep you from him." Her words have a fire brewing in my belly. I have doubts that what she says is true but I need to do my part first.

CHAPTER TWENTY

BEAST

The whole flight all I can picture is her face in the window, it took every ounce of strength I had to turn away from her. She may not know it yet but all of this is for her, to ensure she can get what she wants most. She thinks I haven't noticed but I have. I notice everything about her. She thinks she is clever and that she can fool me. I smile to myself.

Oh, baby, I'm going to shatter your world when I tell you that I know.

The second I land, I check the video surveillance back at Lumiere. When it comes up that the system is offline, I call Chip the second I slide into the back seat of the car with Maurice climbing in next to me.

He answers on the third ring. "You saw?"

I frown. "Saw what? The cameras are down."

He curses beneath his breath and that sets my hackles raising. "Bass... She's gone." My heart begins to pound inside my chest, my blood turning to ice and everything around me becomes white noise. "Bass?"

"When?" I snap.

"Twenty minutes ago."

"I'm on my way," I growl before ending the call. I tell the driver to turn around and take us back.

"What's going on, Bass?" Maurice asks, worry lines dotting his face.

"Bella left," is all I say.

The moon is high in the sky by the time we arrive back at Lumiere, and before we even pull into the drive I can already feel her absence. The last time I pulled in, I felt the warmth of her but this time there is nothing but a dark and empty old church that sits in the distance. The car stops out front of the house. I step out of the car at the same time Chip walks out the front door with a solemn look on his face. I stand here stiff, my muscles are taut to the point of pain.

She left.

I turn away from him and march toward my rose bushes. This time I don't reach for my pruning shears, I just start ripping the flowers from their stems and snapping branches. I don't even feel the bite of the thorns as my rage consumes me. I roar in anger as I destroy the most beautiful things in my life—their beauty fails to compare to hers anyway. She left me for that bastard. I thought she would have fought harder, for herself, for her freedom, for me!

"Bass!" I ignore Maurice and Chip as I continue to destroy the plants that gave my life some beauty. I never should have come out of the fucking shadows! I was safe there, untouchable. Nothing could harm me in the darkness, except she was a bright light that I couldn't hide from. She brought light into my life, I allowed myself to be lulled into the foolish thoughts of her loving me, her accepting me for who I am and what I look like.

"That's enough!" The stern tone of Mrs. Potts's voice is what gets through to me. I stand in the center of my now destroyed rose garden, heaving. Blood drips down my arms and hands but it's what I deserve. I had no business trying to bring her into my world. I keep my back to the others as I drop my chin to my chest and allow the pain that I feel inside to consume me. At least the pain will be a constant reminder that she wasn't a dream, my beauty was real. I've been flayed open by whips, beaten and broken more times than I can even attempt to count but the pain I felt in those moments is nothing compared to the pain I feel now. I feel someone has reached inside my chest and placed a clamp on my heart, slowly tightening it until it breaks.

I feel anger brewing in the pit of my gut. Wanting to feel anything other than this unbearable pain, I latch onto it and use that anger to fuel my revenge. "The plan remains the same. She thinks she can walk away from me and take what is mine with her. I'll show her the real reason I am called the Beast," I snarl.

"Is that... wise?" Mrs. Potts asks hesitantly. I slowly turn around to face them, and each of them tenses when they get a look at me.

"She ran and stole from me. She will go down with the rest of them as soon as I retrieve what is rightfully mine!"

"She gets married in two weeks, Bass. Do think that is enough time to get everything ready?" A dark smirk crosses my face as I look at Chip.

"*I do.*"

Time has rushed by so quickly that we were only able to just to pull everything together in the nick of time. Mrs. Potts will remain behind at Lumiere. Maurice, Chip and I will attend the Masquerade Ball to celebrate the union of Isabella and Gatson—the pompous prick wants a ball the night before his wedding. Everyone knows it's only because he plans to find as many girls as he can to fuck before he is tied to Bella and forced to produce an heir. That thought alone has a smile gracing my face.

These past two weeks feel like they have flown by each day, it's only when night falls that it begins to feel like it's dragging. Lumiere has lost the feeling of warmth it once held when she was within its walls. The place now feels cold, lonely and devoid of any and all love. I peek inside her room every day, her scent still clinging to the air, making me feel like I am close to her again. Mrs. Potts keeps telling me that she didn't leave, that in Bella's own way, she is trying to help. I suspect it was the old woman who disabled to cameras and helped Bella leave. I've yet to find the proof. She may be old but she is fucking sneaky and cunning.

I feel like an idiot as Maurice, Chip and I slip inside the limo, for the sake of appearance we have to arrive like we are somebodies. I have a range of emotions that are currently waring inside me. I'm eager to see Bella and make her pay for thinking she can steal from me and run—she'll learn tonight that I don't take kindly to be made a fool of. Aside from her, the thought of being in the same room as all of those bastards has my skin itching. I want to kill each and every one of them. Maurice says I need to reign in my temper and do things by the book or I risk the lives of everyone I care about. The past two weeks I have come to terms with my decision. I finally feel like I'm making the right choice. I just wanted their deaths and nothing more but now I see in order to really hit them where it hurts, I need to take everything they hold near and dear, and burn it all down while they watch. The thought of them seeing me dismantle their life's work fills me with a sense self-righteousness.

"Are you ready for this?" Chip asks as we exit the gates of Lumiere. I turn my gaze to him. He is going to stand out as he wears a white and gold suit with a mask that matches. His shoes are white with specks of gold glitter.

"I'm ready to ruin everything they hold dear," I answer in a cold tone.

"Tonight, you make your appearance but you do not under any circumstances reveal yourself. We get the layout and the intel we need for tomorrow, then we leave. No distractions," Maurice states. I cut him a glare. I'm the one who calls the shots around here, not him. I let it slide though, knowing how nervous he is about tonight. There is a lot of risk with us showing up there, even though no one will be able to tell who we are, thanks to masks we wear. When Kyran told me about the ball Gatson was hosting, I volunteered to go in his place to get the scope of the land. Maurice and Chip refused to allow me to go alone and decided they would accompany me.

I stare out the window, in less than twenty-four hours the life I have built myself and the life I have lived for the past twenty-eight years is about to change. I may have dreamed of this moment for the past ten years but I never had the... courage to execute the plan until now. I owe this all to the beauty who pulled me from the darkness, only to shred my heart into pieces when she chose to run back to her murderer of a father.

CHAPTER TWENTY-ONE

BELLA

The moment the car pulls up out front of a hotel, the driver carries my bags and leads me to the elevator that takes us to the penthouse. He ushers me inside. I don't get a chance to marvel at the beauty as my grandpa is there and waiting for my arrival. He holds me close and assures me that I will be safe here. I wish his words gave me comfort but they don't. My father would be able to find me within minutes if he wanted to. I tell him everything that I have learned from the books I have read. I'm shocked when I find out that he has known all along. I spend the next couple weeks with grandpa before returning to my father, who is none the wiser that I even left Lumiere. Grandpa and I have devised a plan, all I need to do is play my part. Nerves thrum through me as I pull up to my father's house the day of the ball.

Unlike my grandpa's driver, this driver doesn't carry my bags or lead me inside. I make my way toward the front door which is opened from the inside for me. I mumble my thanks and the moment I step inside I'm stunned. The whole area has been transformed into something out of a fairy tale. Vines are woven through the rails of the staircase, fairy lights are hanging everywhere. I drop my bags at the foot of the stairs as I continue to walk through the house and stare at all the decorations. The one that steals my breath is the dining hall, all the furniture has been removed. Long tables line one side of the wall where there is a massive chocolate fountain and in the far corner, there is a stage set up for a band—holy crap, he has gone all out. Staff rush in and out of the room, hanging ornaments and rearranging the lights, or adding glasses to the table. I slowly back out of the room, not wanting to get in their way. The moment I enter the main foyer, I wished I had stayed in the room.

"My love." I grind my teeth, take a deep breath and force a smile.

"Gatson." I try to sound happy to see him but fall short. He ignores that as he moves toward me and places a chaste kiss to my lips. I'm proud of myself for not gagging.

"Thank goodness you're home." The fact he actually sounds genuinely happy gives me pause. "You have a team of ladies in your room ready to make you presentable. Now don't keep them waiting, I'm sure they will need all the time they can to fix you up." Son of a bitch! I have to bite my tongue to keep from snapping at the arrogant prick. I don't trust myself to speak so I nod, grab my bags and head upstairs. Sure enough the moment I open my bedroom door, I'm greeted with six women and an array of clothes racks. Suitcases litter my floor with makeup, shoes and hair extensions. It takes a second for them to notice me, then they pounce.

For the next six or so hours, I am poked, prodded, waxed against my will and scrubbed clean. I'm not exaggerating, I wasn't allowed to shower alone. They insisted on me hopping in the tub so they could give me a manicure and pedicure as well as treat my hair before the real fun begins as they liked to call it. I'm almost at my wit's end, if one of these women come near me with another pair of tweezers or makeup brush I'm going to punch them in the face. One of them even picked out the thong and strapless bra I'd be wearing tonight. I stand here on a circle podium in nothing but a yellow lace thong and matching bra with yellow heels on.

"The yellow ballgown will make her eyes pop," the brown-haired woman says. The others nod their agreement. Thank God, if they fought over one more thing I would be tempted to just go out there in my undergarments. My bedroom door opens. I squeal in fright and try to find something to cover myself with but it's too late, my father and Gatson have already seen me. I lift my head high and try to act like their presence doesn't matter to me, even though I am practically naked.

Not long, Bella, keep calm and then everything will be fine, as long as they don't notice.

"You will be expected downstairs in an hour, the guest are starting to arrive." I nod.

"Yes, father." Gatson can't seem to take his eyes off my tits that are pushed up so much by this bra they feel like they will hit my chin.

"Don't embarrass me, your grandfather will be here with the elders and you are to stay away from him." I bite my lip to keep my angry retort inside and nod again.

"Yes, father."

"Tomorrow night can't come soon enough," Gatson says in a breathy voice causing the women off to the side to giggle and blush. I stand here trying not to shudder in disgust at the thought of him on top of me.

"Yes, she needs a firm hand so make sure you break her in properly." My nostrils flare in anger at my father's innuendo. I play my part and smile coyly, acting like the thought of him fucking me excites me.

"She'll be broken in *thoroughly*. Then placed on a diet, she seems like she has gained a few pounds." Fucking pig! I hate how my own father stands there and listens to a man speak about his own daughter like she is an animal. The bastard shoots me a wink before he follows my father out of the room. The glam squad leaps into action the moment they leave the room and begin to dress me in a ballgown that weighs a ton! With five minutes to spare the glam team excuse themselves and promise that two of them will help me out of the dress later tonight. I barely hear them leave as I stand here in front of the mirror and look at myself. My makeup isn't thick, it has a natural look to it. My hair is half pinned up in a fancy style bun with beads stitched into it while the rest hangs in loose curls down my back. The yellow ballgown is stunning, the straps rest on the sides of my arms and the bodice digs into my sides making it hard to breathe. It flows out around me, and call me stupid but I feel like a princess in this dress. It's stunning and for the first time, I feel beautiful.

The heels are hard to walk in so I grip the railing as I slowly descend the stairs. When I reach the halfway mark the hairs on the back of my neck stand on end. I dart my eyes around the gathered crowd beneath me all their eyes are on me. I try to find him but then I remind myself, there is no way he would come to this house or much less subject himself to a room full of these people. I push myself to continue down the stairs. Gatson waits at the bottom in a red and black suit-looking thing with a matching mask. He holds his hand out to me. I have to force myself to smile and place my hand in his. He kisses my knuckles, making me want to snatch my hand back but I don't. I allow him to lead me through the crowd of people. I have no idea who any of them even are. Some greet me while others openly leer my way.

We come to a stop in front of a man who reminds me of Gatson, they look like they could be twins. "Father, allow me to introduce you to Isabella Amorro, my intended." My eyes widen slightly, I didn't expect his father to be here tonight. "Isabella, meet my father, LeFou." I smile and bow my head in a show respect. LeFou returns my gesture. Unlike his son, he doesn't give me the creeps or look at me like I'm merely a transaction. I feel Gatson grow tense beside me when his father steps forward, grabs my hand and places a kiss on the top of it.

"It's a pleasure to meet you, Isabella." He releases my hand and I find myself smiling kindly at the man, something about him makes me feel at ease. Grandpa had warned me that a lot of the people here tonight are not what they seem. LeFou cuts his gaze to his son and the relaxed expression he sported when he looked to me is replaced by one of... disgust? "Generations before you made our country proud, you make us weak." My eyes widen to saucers.

"You're not the head of this family any longer, old man," Gatson grits out through clenched teeth. "Excuse us," he snarls before he grips my hand in a vice-like grip that has me flinching as he drags me away. We spend the next couple of hours speaking to people who ignore me for the most part. I don't mind though. I have no idea what they are even droning on about, I'm too busy scanning the crowd. "Of course, Isabella would love to." At the mention of my name, I turn back toward Gatson. He narrows his eyes in warning as an older gentleman steps in front of me and extends his hand.

"May I have this dance?" I fight my groan and smile instead as I place my hand in his. He leads us to the center of the dance floor where other couples dance. "You look very beautiful."

"Thank you," I say on a sigh. He chuckles and I cringe. "Sorry, that was rude." He shakes his head and bends lower until he is able to whisper in my ear.

"He's here, Bella." I reel back and stare up at the older gentleman in a black suit with a black mask that conceals half his face. He smiles and backs away, leaving me confused until I feel *him*. I close my eyes, take a deep breath and muster all the courage inside me as I slowly turn around and come face to face with him. Even with a mask I would know it's him. We stand here staring at each other, my eyes drinking him in. He wears a blue suit, but what catches my eye is the yellow that runs along the lapels of his pedi coat. I trail my gaze lower, he wears black dress pants with a yellow stripe down the side of each leg. I draw my gaze back to his face, his mask only allows the bottom of his face to be seen. The silver mask covers his scars but it still can't mask his beauty. His eyes burn with anger and betrayal, I want to wipe that look away but I can't, not right now.

"You shouldn't be here," I say low enough for only him to hear. He ignores me as he steps forward, and grips my waist drawing a gasp from me. The feeling of his hands on me again after so long has my body spurring to life. I rest my hands on his shoulders as he begins to move us, his eyes never leaving mine. Everything around us fades out as I get lost in his eyes and the feeling of him being this close to me again. I want to say so much to him but I have no idea how or where to even begin. So, I keep my mouth closed and just breathe him in. I don't know how it happened but when the song comes to an end and I slowly blink my eyes open, I realize that I'm resting my cheek against his chest. I quickly step back and dart my gaze around the room. The moment my gaze collides with Gatson's, I know I fucked up. "Shit."

"Run back to your fiancé like the good little dog that you are." I snap my head back toward Bass, his eyes burning with hatred as he stares down at me. I open my mouth to deny his claim but it's too late, he turns and walks toward the exit where the man in the black suit from earlier stands with a guy in a white and gold suit, that's when it all clicks. The man was Maurice and the guy in the sparkly suit that shoots me a wink when they walk out is Chip. What the hell were they doing here?

The rest of the night drags on. Gatson doesn't leave my side for a second after seeing me on the dance floor with Bass, he hasn't even said a word about it which worries me more. I can't afford for him to hurt me. He may not have said anything and keeps a smile on his face but I can feel the tension wafting off him in waves. I'm exhausted, my feet hurt and I really need to pee but there is no way I can manage that feat by myself in this dress. I pay no attention to any of the conversations he has, not even when my father joins us. Another hour passes and I can't take it, I need to pee so badly, I gently grip his arm and act as if I just want to place a kiss to his cheek but instead whisper in his ear. It grates on my nerves to ask permission but I know if I do it, it will inflate his ego and he'll be more likely to let me go without a fuss.

"May I be excused? It's been such a long night and I have preparations to make for tomorrow, *my love*." I nearly gag saying that part. When he reels back and stares at me with wide eyes, I keep the doe-eyed look on my face and smile sweetly. He recovers quickly and smiles invitingly as he leans in. I know he is about to kiss me so I force myself to remain still. The moment his lips touch mine a shudder rolls through me, he mistakes that for need. The truth is I shudder with disgust. He pulls back and nods his approval.

"Of course, my love. You definitely need your beauty sleep." The men around us chuckle as I force a smile and nod. "Off you go, this is no conversation for a woman anyhow." I thank him and bid the men goodbye, hating how their gazes are fixated on my tits. I rush from the room and practically run up the stairs to my bedroom, throw the door open and sigh appreciatively at the sight of the two ladies.

"Get me out of this thing, now!" I snap. They rush to me and begin to undo the corset lace at the back, I'm jumping on the spot about to piss myself when the bloody garment finally falls to the ground. I race to the bathroom and slam the door. I relieve myself and my God, it is the best feeling in the world. After flushing, I stand in front of the sink in my bathroom, wash my hands and then stare at myself in the mirror. I turn sideways and bite down on my lip, before tearing my gaze from the mirror and heading back into my room. A grateful sigh leaves me when I find the room empty and the dress nowhere in sight. I stand at the end of my bed in nothing but my bra, thong and yellow heels, exhausted and ready to call it a night. My breath hitches as the lights go out and the hairs on the back of my neck stand on end.

He's here.

CHAPTER TWENTY-TWO

BEAST

She knows I'm here. I see it in the way her body relaxes and her breaths come in fast pants as excitement begins to build inside her. Months ago she was scared of what lurked in the dark but now, she begs for what the darkness hides. The dim lighting of the moon that peaks through her window gives me a clearer view of her. Her back is to me with the globes of her ass on display. Fuck, the sight of her in that yellow bra and thong has my cock growing hard. When my gaze trails lower and I spot the heels, I nearly groan out loud. I watch as she lifts her arms and removes the pins that keep her hair in place—she knows I love tugging on her long locks while I fuck her. She chucks the pins to the side and drops her arms back to her sides. I move in closer until I am pressed against her back, a soft moan tumbles from her lips as she leans back into me. I want to shove her but I would be lying if I said I didn't love the way she knows it's me without even having to see me.

"Don't be angry with me," she whispers, the sound of her voice has my anger peaking. I reach around and grip her throat, she doesn't fight me as I tighten my hold and force her head until she looks up at me. The happiness I see in her eyes at the sight of me has me wanting to break her apart until she is nothing but pieces, exactly like my heart. I slip my other hand around her and lay it flat against her stomach, her breath stills, that's all the confirmation I need.

"You thought you could run from me, take what is *mine* and that I would what? Go back to hiding in the shadows while you passed *my* kid off as your future husband's heir?" Her eyes widen, the look of happiness is replaced with fear, not for herself but for the child she carries inside her.

"Bass... I... it's not—"

"Shut the fuck up, Bella!" I snap in a cold emotionless tone that has her eyes filling with moisture. "Save your tears for someone who fucking cares. You pulled me from the darkness, made me come into the light and live again only to run from me the first chance you got. I should have known you were exactly like your father, you'll do anything to win." Her eyes blaze with loathing. She begins to struggle in my hold but I'm stronger than her. When she begins to get really worked up I use the grip I have on her throat and force her backward until she falls on the bed. I straddle her legs, careful not to move any higher and put pressure on her stomach. She lashes out and manages to slap me across the face. I growl before I grip both her wrists in one hand and pin them above her head as I get right in her face.

"Fuck you! I fucking hate you," she snarls. I smile right in her face, knowing it will piss her off.

"I fucking hate you too!" She recoils, pressing further into the bed, her eyes search my face for any sign of deceit.

"Then why the fuck are you here? Did you come to fuck me again and then break my heart as you leave me broken and alone on the shower floor?" Her words are coated with such bitterness that I almost feel bad for her, until I remember what she tried to take from me!

"If I wanted to fuck you, we both know you would open your legs willingly for me, so don't play coy."

She scoffs. "The sight of you makes me drier than a humid summer in Florida." I quirk a brow in challenge. She stiffens beneath me the moment I release her throat and trail my hand down her body. When my fingers brace over the lace that covers her pussy, she sucks in a sharp intake of air. "Get your hands off me!" she grits out. I slip my hand inside her panties.

"You're a bad liar," I mock as I slip a finger through her folds, my gaze snapping to hers. She turns her head away from me as I smirk. She is fucking soaked. Unable to restrain myself, I force a finger inside her and relish in the whimper that tumbles from her lips. "Do you get wet for everyone you hate or am I just lucky?" She slowly turns her head back toward me, the sight of her tears running down her cheeks gives me pause.

"I wish I hated you," she whispers brokenly as the tears flow faster down her cheeks. I remove my hand from her panties and release my hold on her wrists as I slump back on my haunches, keeping my face blank of all emotion. "I want to hate you so badly but... I can't because I love you too fucking much. You ruined everything! I was fine before you claimed me. I felt nothing, wanted nothing and was happy to live a loveless life until the day I died. You made me want things, feel things I had no right to feel. Even when you left me broken and alone in that shower weeks ago, I had no idea at the time, but I wasn't really alone, I had a part of you inside me." The slight lilt of happiness in her tone angers me further.

"And yet you still chose to run from me with that knowledge! If I find out you have fucked him while pregnant with my child, I'll not only snap his fucking neck, I'll snap yours the second after you give birth."

Her eyes narrow as she shakes her head in annoyance. "I didn't arrive here until this morning, you asshole and just to clear this fucking thing up, this is *my* baby as well. You so much as try to take her from me and I'll make you hiding in the shadows seem like a daydream." My brows raise at the fierce protectiveness in her tone.

"*Her?*" She nibbles on her bottom lip and darts her gaze away from me. I grip her chin and force her eyes back to mine. She sighs before answering.

"I don't know if it's a girl, I just kind of have a feeling."

"You say you love me, yet you take one of the most precious gifts I would ever receive in this life from me, why?" It shocks the hell out of me when she reaches up and cups my face between her hands. I should pull away but the feeling of her hands on me after so long feels too fucking good.

"I never ran from you, Bass. I left for a short while to ensure I was able to return to you. Even if you don't love me, I was always coming back to you to share this amazing news." I frown.

"Where the hell did you go if you weren't here?"

"My grandpa's."

I tense. "Why?"

She smiles lovingly up at me. "I happened to find out that the true heir to the family is still alive, a Vital heir lives, Bass *'If the intended shall fail to marry their chosen, the heir to the prior Don will be accepted as replacement. The intended must decree in front of the old families, the new, their intended and the prior heir. The intended may never be swayed by the previous heir, all must be the choice of the intended. The heir may never reveal who they are or which family they belong to. From the moment of the lockout, the clock will start, allowing the intended three months to change their mind."* She recites the verse that I know better than anyone back to me, like I haven't a clue what it means.

"So, what's your plan? Find the Vital heir, choose him and what?"

She darts her tongue out to moisten her lips as she stares into my eyes. "Hope to God that he will choose me and love me too."

"You think you love someone you've never met all because a fucking book says you should?" I snap angrily. Her hold on my face tightens as she pulls me down to her so our noses are touching.

"I've met him and I need him to know, I choose him because I love him not because he is my second choice but because he is my *only* choice. I ran from you when I found those books in your room because I needed to know if what I found is the truth and if I could pull it off. I found that I can, but the rules state that the heir must choose me as well." She sucks in a deep breath as her eyes bore into mine. "Do you, Bastian Vital, choose me?"

I suck in a sharp intake of breath at hearing my real name tumble from her lips. I close my eyes and rest my forehead against hers. "You know?"

"I do and I am so sorry. I wish I could change what happened to you. I fucking hate them for what they put you through and if you accept me, I swear to fucking God I will stand before those elders tomorrow and rat that bastard out. You have nothing to fear now. They can't harm you, Bass. My grandfather has been trying to find you since the moment he realized your body was never accounted for. He covered that up in the hopes you were rescued. He wants you to lead the family. He can't outright overthrow my father but together, we can dethrone the son of a bitch who took everything from you!"

"How did you know about the books, Bella?" She at least has the decency to look sheepish as she answers.

"I overheard you and Chip one night arguing about them." I take a deep breath and try to reign in my annoyance. "The day you left, I went to the west wing and found them."

"That door was locked," I hedge. She flicks her gaze to the side but at the sound of my growl she snaps it back to me.

"Promise you won't be mad?" I narrow my eyes. "Mrs. Potts gave me the key, she also turned the cameras off so you wouldn't know what I was up to." I shake my head, I fucking knew it was her that disabled the cameras. "Why didn't you tell me?" I eye her warily, not sure if should I trust her with this information.

"Why didn't you tell me you were pregnant?" She sucks a sharp breath in and turns away from me. "Yeah, that's exactly what I thought. I'm okay to fuck you but the thought of having a child with me puts you off." Her head snaps back to me, fire burns in her eyes.

"Get the fuck off me, Bass." Bending down I nip at the side of her neck before licking a trail to the shell of her ear. She tries to fight the shiver that courses through her.

"You know it gets me hard when you fight me, Beauty," I whisper in her ear.

"Well, you're not fucking me!" she snarls, but her words

lack heat. I lick along her jawline, stopping when I reach her lips, her eyes blazing with lust.

"You're the only one I'll be fucking, Beauty. Deny it all you want but you want me as much as I fucking crave you." I shift slightly so I can run my hand down her side, ghosting my fingers over the top of her thong, I press my finger against her clit, relishing in the heady groan that forces it's way past her lips. I glide my finger lower and growl when I feel that she has soaked through her panties. "Your pussy never lies," I say huskily.

"I... I can't." I cup her pussy as I hold her gaze. "I'm in love with you, Bastian. My heart can't take you only wanting me because of the baby. I never should have hidden the pregnancy from you but I didn't see another way. I wanted so badly to find a way to be with you and have *our* baby. I did that, except I know what I want... And what I want is a life with you and our child. Nothing about you puts me off, every single thing about you, scars and all, just makes me love you harder. You don't see your beauty because you never come into the light. Let me be the light to show you that you are beautiful. You're not a beast, maybe in the bedroom but not in your heart."

I push her panties to the side and slip a finger inside her, loving how her mouth parts slightly and her eyes flicker. I press my lips against hers as I work my finger in and out of her. We never break eye contact, even when I kiss her again. It hits me then, Bella is mine and she needs to know it. I keep pumping into her as I speak.

"You are mine." A whimper escapes her. "Every single part of you belongs to me. I'm the only one who will ever get to see you come. I've lived in the darkness my whole life until you came to me. I know I'm in love with you because I'd rather not sleep and dream, my reality is better than any dream because of you. I love you, Isabella Amorro." Tears leak from her eyes, she grips my face and smashes her lips against mine, pouring all her love into this kiss, showing me the only way we both know how to express ourselves, through touch. I withdraw my finger and yank her panties off. She moans into my mouth when I nudge her legs apart without breaking our kiss.

CHAPTER TWENTY-THREE

BELLA

I feel his love for me in this kiss, but hearing him utter those three little words has my heart expanding to the point I fear it might burst. He reaches under me to unclasp my bra. The moment he chucks the thing to the side, his hands are cupping my tits. He groans into my mouth. I don't know how the fuck he got in here, but I am so glad he did because we both needed this. I grip the hem of his hoodie and pull that and his shirt over his head. He breaks our kiss to help me but then his lips are sealed against mine within a second. I get to work on undoing his jeans. He growls when he's forced to shuffle off the bed to rid himself of his pants. I lift my head and smirk at the sight of his cock, hard and ready for me.

He slowly climbs on top of me, resting his elbows on either side of my face and kisses me as he slowly pushes inside me. I whimper into his mouth, it's been weeks since he's been in me. Fuck, it stings slightly as he slowly pushes inside me, but I don't care about the pain. I need this, I need to feel him and know that we are one. The moment he is fully sheathed inside me we both groan. He breaks our kiss and holds my gaze as he slowly rocks his hips. My eyes fight to close but I don't allow it. He has never made love to me before, he's always been rough, hard and demanding but tonight, he's showing me without words that he truly does love me.

"Bass," I moan when he hits that sweet spot inside me. He captures my lips to swallow my cries as he continues to fuck me at a steady pace—it's driving me crazy! I can feel my orgasm building but it's just out of reach. I break the kiss much to his dismay. "I need you to fuck me hard!" I practically growl. He quirks a brow in surprise and stops moving.

"Is... is that safe for the... baby?" Oh God, my heart melts inside my chest.

"The baby is fine, you won't hurt it." I reassure him with a smile. He nods but I can see from the look in his eyes he still isn't convinced. "I promise, the baby will be fine but I won't be if you don't fuck me like the beast I know you are." His eyes darken, he pushes back and lifts one of my legs to rest against his shoulder, he lays his hand flat on my other leg to keep it flat against the bed as he pushes forward. A gasp tumbles from my lips. He's so fucking deep that I swear I can feel him in my stomach. He thrusts inside me and I cry out, loving how he can go from tender and sweet to a fucking savage in seconds.

"Grab that pillow, bite down on it. I can't have your father hearing me fuck his daughter just yet." I'm so fucking sick in the head, I grab the pillow above my head and bite down on it. I don't know what the hell is wrong with me, the thought of my father hearing me scream and the prospect of him catching me with Bass excites me. "You like that, Beauty?" I moan into the pillow as he continues to pump in and out of me. "You want Daddy to hear you coming all over my cock, don't you?" My response is to moan when he hits my G-spot again. "What if Daddy saw me eating your ass, you think he knows his baby girl likes taking my cock in her ass?" His dirty words are my undoing, I come so fucking hard and scream so loud that Bass is forced to push the pillow harder against my mouth to muffle my screams. His pace intensifies as he chases his own release. I feel him swelling inside me except before he can come he pulls out of me. My leg falls from his shoulder as he grips the back of my neck with his free hand and continues to pump his cock with the other. He pulls me into a half-sitting position, and not a second later he bites down on his bottom lip to keep quiet as he spurts jets of come all over my tits and face. I gasp when I feel his come sliding down my cheek.

Feeling emboldened and a tiny bit naughty, I hold his gaze as I reach up and use my index finger to swipe the cum from my cheek. I bring that finger to my mouth and suck it clean, moaning the second I taste him on my tongue. His eyes blaze, I know that look, Bass is far from done with me and I just know he is going to fuck me until the sun rises and I can't wait. I want to be covered from head to toe in his cum as I stand before the elders, my father and Gatson when I tell them I choose Bass. I pray that Gatson and my father will be able to see that I'm marked and owned by Bastian Vital.

"I want your cum all over me. I want them all to know who I belong to when I walk into that room tomorrow and announce that I choose you!" It's like my words snap something inside him, he pounces on me, his worry for the baby forgotten for the moment as he ravishes my body all night long marking me in every way possible. Our need for each other is insatiable, we can't keep our hands to ourselves. We finally manage to sleep as the sun rises. Bass refuses to remove his cock from inside me. Too exhausted to argue with him, that's how I fall asleep.

The sound of banging on the door rouses me from my slumber. I shout for whoever it is to go away but when the sound of his voice registers, I practically leap out of the bed with my heart in my throat. I look around the room and frown, Bass is nowhere to be seen. Where is he?

"Isabella!" my father shouts. I shake my head and pull myself together.

"I've just showered, Father, I will be there in a moment," I call back, hoping he buys my lie.

"You have twenty minutes, your ladies in waiting were... held up." I roll my eyes. What he means to say is they are in Gatson's bed and that's where they spent the night after they helped me from my dress.

"That's okay, I'll be ready shortly."

"Don't fuck this up," he warns before I hear his footsteps fading away down the hallway. Only then do I release the breath I didn't know I was holding. I rush into my closet and bathroom, my hope dwindles when I find them both empty. Was last night a dream? The ache between my legs tells me it wasn't, then why would he leave? I push away those thoughts as I rush around and get myself ready, forgoing a shower. I brush my teeth and run a comb through my hair deciding to leave it down, knowing it will piss Gatson off. Just as I leave the bathroom my phone begins to ring, it's from an unknown number. I answer it anyway, just to give me something else to think about instead of what waits for me downstairs. I am to pass the test this morning and then tonight, I'm to be married before the elders.

"Hello?" I sound deflated.

"Why so sad my beauty?" My eyes widen as a whoosh of air escapes me at the sound of his voice.

"Because you weren't here when I woke up," I answer honestly.

"Tomorrow, the next day and every day after that you'll be waking up next to me." Hope builds inside me.

"Where are you?"

"Bella, do you trust me?" I don't even hesitate.

"Yes."

"Then trust me when I tell you that I will be there. You won't see me but just know I have everything covered. They will never get the chance to ever hurt you again."

"Promise me you meant what you said last night?" I drop down onto the edge of my bed and wait with bated breath for him to answer me.

"I meant every word. I'm coming for you and our baby, speak your truth and I swear to you, Beauty, I'll be watching your back the whole time." My father calls my name from outside my door, nerves thrum through me.

"I love you, my Beast," I whisper.

"I love you, my Beauty." God, hearing those words from him has a renewed sense of determination flowing through me. I end the call, and run my hands down my cream-colored blouse that I paired with a gray Gucci pencil skirt and Jimmy Choo nude pumps. I make my way out of my room to find my father standing there with an angry look on his face. The sight of him fills me with disgust. How he can stand the sight of himself in the mirror each day astounds me—he murdered an entire family, *children*! Oh God, my stomach rolls at the thought of him ever harming Bass, I would never survive that.

"You *will* pass this test. Tonight after the marriage is complete you will make sure that the shares in the US are turned over to me. I don't care if you have to let him tear your ass open to get me what I want, you will do it, am I clear?" I keep my face slack but make sure he can see the hatred in my eyes as I answer.

"Crystal." He takes a step forward but is halted at the sound of my grandpa's voice.

"My sweet girl, it's been too long." My father's face turns red. I pull my gaze from him and act the part.

"Grandpa, I've missed you." We embrace each other in a hug, then my father storms down the stairs muttering under his breath. My grandpa pulls back and rests his hands on my shoulders, darts his gaze around making sure we are alone before he speaks.

"Tell them exactly what you told me, that's it." I nod.

"He won't let me go, my father won't take losing well."

"Your father has no choice, I may not have the power to overthrow him but even the members of the elders that he has bought can't argue when you have the proof."

"Grandpa, I have to tell you something–" He smiles adoringly.

"You have the same glow your mother did when she was pregnant with you." My jaw slackens causing him to chuckle. "I may be old but I'm not blind." His eyes shine with nothing but love. "You *both* will be safe after today, I will make sure of it."

It amazes me how fast the staff was able to transform the ballroom. Instead of the fairy tale vibe from last night, it's set out like a board room. A large oval table in the center that could easily seat twenty people, Grandpa and the six other elders sit at one end of it. My father and Gatson stand off to the side, leaning against the wall, each of them shoots me a scathing look. I release a nervous breath and walk toward the seat at the far end of the table, the only sound that can be heard in the room are my heels clicking against the hardwood floors. I take my seat and run my gaze over each of the elders. They are all older gentlemen, none of them wear a suit like my father and Gatson. Don't get me wrong, I can tell their clothing is designer but they dress casually. From left to right each of them introduces themselves.

"I am, Antonio." I nod politely and smile as the man next to him speaks.

"I'm Rafe." They continue around the table until they reach my grandfather, he smiles at me and winks.

"No introductions need be made here." I and the other six men chuckle lightly. Grandpa straightens in his seat, his eyes harden and a mask of indifference slips across his face as he looks at me. "Isabella Amorro, daughter of Don Phillipe Amorro, you have been summoned here by the elder council to retell the history of the families and answer any questions that are asked of you. If you fail, your father is free to exact any punishment he sees fit for you bringing shame upon your family. Do you understand?"

I swallow audibly. "Yes, I understand." I'm proud that my voice doesn't waiver. Rafe clears his throat drawing my attention to him, his eyes hold no kindness only malice and I know instantly he is one of the elders on my father's payroll.

"Isabella Amorro, recite to me the history of the Amorro

family." I nod, this one is easy. I tell them how my father worked in my grandfather's organization, married my mother and took over as the head of my grandfather's family once he was elected to serve on the council. "What position does your intended hold in his family?" I frown, it was never mentioned that I would need to learn of Gatson's family.

"I'm sorry, I wasn't aware that my intendeds position or his family history would be part of this." I make sure to keep my gaze on Rafe and not allow it to stray to my grandfather.

"It is not. This is a first time event for us all, the lockout has always been about the history of our families." Palo, states from across the table shooting Rafe a warning look.

"If our family is to be interconnected with the Polish, is it not wise that she be able to speak on both side's history?" Claud, who sits next to Rafe fires back.

"Enough!" Donny, the man who sits in the middle at the other end of the table says whilst keeping his gaze on me. There is a power that clings to him, you can feel it. I know without a doubt he is the head of the elders. "Isabella Amorro, I am told that you have information that pertains to the families. I'm also led to believe that what you have to say will rock the foundation we have built over the past decades." I gulp and nod, his eyes crinkle at the corners. "Speak, child, and make sure what you have to say is the truth for your life and many others depend on it."

Before I can utter a word my father rushes froward with an angry look directed my way. "Isabella, you are not to speak out of turn. Just answer the questions asked, you know nothing and are wasting the time of very important men!" he snarls at me. I look up at my father and slowly climb to my feet, I run my gaze over the sorry excuse of a human and shake my head.

"You have no power here, *Father*," I spit the word at him

like it burns my tongue. His eyes blaze and his nostrils flare as he takes a single step toward me only halting at the sound of Grandpa's voice.

"You will remain silent and return to your post. Isabella has invoked the right of *Sanctum.*" The look in my father's eyes has me wanting to cower but I stand tall, refusing to allow him to bully me any longer. I hold his gaze with a firm look of my own until he is forced to break our stare off and return to his spot next to a worried looking Gatson. "You have the floor," Grandpa says. I hold my head high and straighten my shoulders as I speak.

"I, Isabella Amorro, have completed the mandatory lockout that is enforced by the elder council. During the lockout, I learned of a key piece of information that my own father had hidden from me."

"What information?" Donny asks, meeting his gaze as I speak.

"I am here to decree before my father, my intended and the elder council that I hereby profess my refusal to marry Gatson Kaluza." Gasps ring out around the room but I push on refusing to be deterred. "I hereby put forward my marriage to the *true* heir of the families."

"She has lost her fucking mind!" Gatson shouts. Chaos ensues as everyone begins to shout and demand answers. My father storms over to me, grips me roughly by the arm and tries to yank me out of the room. My grandpa leaps to his feet, ready to intervene but the moment Donny stands everything comes to a stop, even my father stops dragging me the moment his voice breaks through.

"Sit the hell down now! Phillipe, release the child now and resume your post. If you move again, you will be removed from the room! Everyone will remain silent and allow the child to speak or you will be dismissed and the decision will lay with me alone." My father snarls, then releases me with a hard shove. I stumble backward, my heels slip along the hardwood and I cry out as I fall backward. Before I can hit the hard floor hands grip my waist, my body burns with awareness, the hairs on the nape of my neck stand on end as I'm placed back on my feet. My back pressed against his chest.

"You ever touch her again and I'll tear your fucking throat out." The promise in his words sends a shiver down my spine. My father and Gatson dart their gazes between me and Bass, their confusion is clear on their faces.

"What the hell is the meaning of this?" Palo demands.

"Tell them the truth, Bella," Bass rasps out. I ignore everyone else in the room except for Donny, I meet his hardened stare as I say.

"The last two weeks of my lockout were not spent at Lumiere." My father tries to butt in but one look from Donny has him silenced, so I continue. "I discovered in the books that there was an unsanctioned mass murder of the Vital family." I cut my gaze to my father as I say. "Phillipe Amorro thought he had killed every living Vital, which meant he would become the head of the family. Except you were wrong... One heir lives and he's ready to claim his place as the rightful Don!" I turn back to Donny. "I was never swayed by anyone at Lumiere, in fact, books were hidden from me so I wouldn't discover the truth but I found a way. Once I found the proof, I called for help and was able to find proof of what was written in the books. I, Isabella Amorro, hereby offer a union of peace between the Vital and Amorro family to try make amends for what my father did."

Donny looks to each of the other elders before turning

his stunned gaze back to me. "Miss Amorro, the accusations you have made—"

I cut in. "What I say is the truth. I have proof!"

"If you have proof, then where is this Vital heir you speak of?" Bass moves to stand beside me. I see out of the corner of my eye that he isn't alone, Chip, Maurice and at least a dozen other men are here that are all dressed like they are in the military.

"I would think after selling out the Don to the Vital family that maybe your conscious would have gotten the better of you, Rafe." I manage to school my features and keep the shock from my face at Bass's confession.

CHAPTER TWENTY-FOUR

BASTIAN

The bastard, Rafe tries to hide his horror but fails. "Who the hell are you?" he snaps, trying to deflect. I turn my gaze to Phillipe and hold his stare as I answer.

"I am Bastian Vital, the only living heir to the Vital family." Shouts erupt but I block them out as I watch Phillipe's face slowly morph into disbelief.

"What proof do you have of your identity?" Bella's grandfather asks. Maurice steps forward holding the manila envelope.

"Take a good look at me, Mikale, I'm sure you would be able to remember your old friend?" Phillipe turns pale at the sight of Maurice. Mikale's eyes widen.

"Maurice?" he breathes out.

"Hello, old friend," Maurice says before he turns to the head of the council–Donny. "I was the second in charge to Antonio Vital. I was the one who rescued the boy and hid him at Lumiere while I ran from Amorro's men for the better part of a decade. I was unable to supply the council with proof at the time, due to not being sure if Mikale would protect his son-in-law." Bella's grandfather looks appalled. "I have here the birth certificate of Bastian Vital. I also have letters from myself that I left with Father Cogsworth at Lumiere to be given to Bass when he was of age. I also have all the books of the Vital's history here with me, that I wrote." Bella gasps beside me. I wrap my arm around her waist and whisper low enough for only her to hear.

"Maurice was my father's best friend and the one tasked with noting our family history." Maurice hands the envelope to Donny before coming back to stand by me. Minutes tick by as Donny goes through the paperwork and passes it to the other members.

"You can't do this, you have broken the rules and told the girl who you are, what family you came from. The lockout states—"

"You don't fucking speak to me!" I roar. Rafe recoils, then quickly rights himself but I have garnered the attention of all the members now. "The entire church is fitted with surveillance. I have every encounter with Bella documented as proof that nothing was said and she was never pointed in the direction to discover my true identity. If you need the proof, I'll happily supply it for you–" I turn my gaze to Gatson as I say the last part with a smile on my face. "But, you may want to forward through some of it because I'm sure none of you want to see Bella riding my cock or screaming my name." Gatson's eyes widen, his face turns red as his anger begins to peak knowing I've been fucking her for months.

"If what you say is true," I look back to the elders and hold Palo's gaze as he speaks, "that no one has told her who you are, how then does she know?" Bella steps forward to answer for me.

"Bass locked away the books that exposed his identity in his room. I broke in and found them. Plus, he admitted it to me last night while he was fucking me senseless in celebration of my news."

"What fucking news?" Gatson snaps, moving until he stands on the other side of the table opposite us. I shift behind Bella and wrap my arms around her waist and lay my hand flat against her stomach.

"The news of our pregnancy of course," she says in an overly sweet voice that is filled with mockery.

"You fucking bitch—" Gatson doesn't have a chance to finish that insult, I pull the gun from my waistband and plant a bullet in the middle of his forehead. Bella screams as the elders begin to try and run, but Kyran and his men stop their exit. I watch as the bastard drops to the floor with blood running from the hole in the center of his forehead.

"You cannot—" I point my gun at Rafe which has him clamping his mouth closed. Donny steps forward pinning me with a stern look, I slowly lower my gun but don't holster it.

"You just started a war, boy," Donny states in a matter of fact tone of voice.

"Actually, I have it in writing from Gatson's father that no action will be taken against the families if I end his son's life as long as it is done before he is married." Chip rushes forward and hands Donny the letter I managed to get from Kaluza last night, he was more than happy to be rid of his son.

"Explain how this has happened, your life depends on it," Donny demands. I smirk.

"From where I'm standing, it looks like I'm the one who has the power to determine the outcome of this situation." Donny narrows his eyes but says nothing, knowing he is outmanned here. "Amorro murdered my family. The books Maurice have proven that. I was raised at Lumiere by Cogsworth who tortured the fuck out of me daily. He is no longer breathing in case you were wondering. Maurice came back when I was ten and tried to help me but Cogsworth threatened to rat us out to Phillipe. When I turned eighteen, I discovered the proof of my birth and the letters. I killed Cogsworth that night and took over Lumiere. I never planned to come back into the fold but then..." Before I can finish coming up with the right words, Mikale butts in.

"My granddaughter was sent to Lumiere for the lock-out." I nod stiffly. "I always hoped that you survived as no body was ever found. I prayed by some miracle that you were out there and would set my Bella free from this marriage. I never banked on her finding you and falling in love." I can hear the love in his tone which shocks me.

"Yes. Bella changed my course of action and I was forced from hiding to claim what is rightfully mine," I growl. Donny nods and turns to face Phillipe, who is standing between two of Kyran's men looking pissed as hell.

"Do you have anything to say for yourself?" Donny asks.

"The boy is lying and clearly being put up to it by the girl. She must have a golden cunt for him–" I don't let the cunt finish speaking, I pull the trigger and shoot him right between the eyes. He goes down like the sack of shit he is. This time, Bella doesn't scream and the council doesn't try to escape.

"Maurice has a recording of the night my father and brother were executed with Amorro admitting to being the one pulling the trigger. As the laws of the families state, I am well within my rights to execute the man who harmed my family." Maurice attempts to step forward with the tape but Donny raises his hand halting him.

"You seem like you have more to add?" I smirk, clever man.

"Three of your council members, Palo, Rafe and Chino were all aware of the murder of my family." The three of them rebuke my claims but I push on. "I have a paper trail of them receiving a wire transfer from Amorro monthly. There is also another tape that we acquired of Amorro naming them as accomplices in aiding him to take out my family." Donny says nothing as he pulls his phone from his pocket dials a number and then snaps.

"Get in here now!" Not a minute later the room is filled with Donny's men. He holds my gaze as he barks out his orders. "Take, Chino, Rafe and Palo back to the house and strap them down." The three men fight and spew about how I am a liar but Donny ignores them, never breaking eye contact with me. Only when they are dragged from the room does he speaks again. "I'll need that proof. I also need assurances that once those three are dealt with that their families will be spared if it is proven they are innocent." Maurice reaches forward and hands one of Donny's men the tapes.

"You have my word that if their families are proven to have had nothing to do with my family's death, then they are free to live," I answer honestly.

"In order to rule as the head Don, you will need to follow the rules," he states.

I nod. "I'm aware. I plan to have those taken care of this evening."

"I'll leave Mikale here as a witness." I nod my agreement. Donny closes the space between us. I feel everyone in the room grow tense until Donny extends his hand toward me. I eye it for a second before placing mine in his to shake. "I knew your father, he was a good man. I hope you will follow in his footsteps." Shocked into silence I just nod. "For what it's worth, had I known that your father was ambushed like he was, I would have dealt with this years ago and raised you with my own sons." My eyes widen slightly before I school my features and watch as he and the others exit the room. His men carry both Gatson and Phillipe's bodies from the room to dispose of. I watch Bella to see if she will react to seeing the lifeless bodies of her father and *ex-fiancé,* but she doesn't bat an eye.

Not wanting to spend another second in that fucking house, I lead Bella out of there with Chip, Maurice and her grandfather trailing after us. Kyran asked me on our way out what I wanted done with the house. It shocked me when Bella answered, saying she wanted her things from her room and then for the house to be burnt to the ground. I gave the okay for them to pack her shit and do as she said, but we didn't stick around to watch the show. The five of us sit in the limo that leads us back to Lumiere. Bella snuggles into my side, gripping the front of my hoodie. I spy her grandfather across from us, staring.

"I'm happy to put a bullet in your head if you have a problem," I growl at the old fucker. Bella gasps and swats me on the chest, earning a glare from me.

"That's my grandpa!" she exclaims.

"And I don't give a shit!" I growl, ready to force her into

submission in front of the others if I have to, but her grandfather's laughter distracts us both. We each look at him confused as to why he is laughing.

"Grandpa, are you okay?" Bella asks cautiously. I roll my eyes, praying the fucker has a heart attack so I don't have to deal with him any longer.

"You two are going to have a long and happy life together." My upper lip lifts in a snarl, he shakes his head and shoots me a... proud look. "You are the challenge she will need to keep her sharp and she is the fire that will never dim when your darkness tries to overthrow her light. You will learn to balance each other out." He shifts his gaze directly to me and I tense ready to fight if I need to. "Bella told me a lot about you while she stayed with me. You helped her see what I couldn't." He tone holds regret but it piques my curiosity which is why I ask.

"How so?" His eyes soften as he looks at my girl. My hold on her tightens, grandfather or not I don't like him looking at her like that.

"I tried to show her there was more to life than obeying her father but failed." He flicks his gaze back to me. "You managed to do what I could not, for that I am indebted to you, Bastian Vital." Hearing my name said out loud has pride swelling inside me. I've never used my full name, not even after Cogsworth was dealt with. My beauty is the reason why I did this but now that it has been done, I realize I didn't just do it for her, I did it for me as well. "At least when she is wed tonight it is to someone she loves."

"*What?*" I smirk when I see the shocked look on her face.

"You were the one who suggested peace through a union," I deadpan.

"I didn't mean tonight!" I grip her face between my

hands and smash my lips to hers, uncaring that the others are watching. When I pull back, she is panting and breathless. Her eyes are glazed over with need, forcing a smile to my face.

"You will be Isabella Vital by the end of the night and you will say *I do* because you and I both know you want this... Shit, you probably want it more than me." Her whole face softens as a coy smile graces her beautiful face.

"I knew we had to marry tonight." she says with laughter clear in her tone. I frown at her.

"What?" She rolls her eyes playfully as she grips the front of my hoodia pulling me to her until her lips ghost over mine.

"I just wanted to hear you say you wanted me just as much as I want you." I am powerless to stop the laughter that breaks free from me.

EPILOGUE

BASTIAN

Thirteen years later...

"Daddy!" I fight back the fucking groan that wants to break free as I slowly twirl around in my chair. I cut my gaze to my wife who stands behind our daughter with a stern look on her face. I shoot her a scathing look. "Please!" I take a deep breath as I look at my little girl who is the spitting image of her mother, with long brown hair, crystal green eyes that shine with nothing but happiness and love. She has my lips and lashes but that's it. I'm not even mad about it. She is the center of my world and I will fucking kill anyone who ever tries to harm my baby.

"Why can't you just stay here and watch it?" I plead. She places her hands on her hips and looks to her mother with a pleading look. Bella pins me with a look that says I need to relax. I throw my hands in the air, fucking annoyed that they are ganging up on me, again!

"Bass, she is just going with Oliver and his mom to watch a movie and then she will be home by four this afternoon." I glare at Bella.

"She's twelve! She should be playing with Barbies and fucking braiding hair not going to the movies with boys!" A knock sounds and I look to my open office door to see Mrs. Potts standing there with a smile on her face. I throw my hands in the air. "Did you all fucking know about this?"

"Don't be angry, Maurice and I offered to ask on her behalf, even Chip offered but she refused and said she wouldn't have anyone else do her dirty work. Kind of sounds like a young boy I know." I shoot Mrs. Potts a scathing look and she laughs me off. "Oliver and his mother are downstairs." I leap to my feet ready to go beat the shit out of a little boy. Bella and Audrey rush me and push me back until I drop into my seat again.

Bella steps between my open legs and pushes Audrey behind her. "Darling, say goodbye to your father and close the door on your way out." My eyes widen. I attempt to stand again but my dirty little minx of a wife anticipates my move and is quick to straddle my lap keeping me in place. "Let her go have and fun and I might just let you have some fun." My eyes bore into Bella's to find them filled with longing.

"Oh, that is gross!" my daughter admonishes. I turn to her and try to pin her with a glare but I can never manage to look at her with anything but love. Her mother may have tamed the beast inside me but she causes it to disappear.

"Back by four, Audrey." She squeals but I'm not finished. "If Oliver even attempts to hold your hand or breathe the same air as you, I'll make sure we hold his funeral service in this church." Her jaw drops. I puff my chest out, feeling satisfied I managed to one up my twelve-year-old daughter.

"Go! Quick before he changes his mind," Bella practically shouts. Audrey rushes to leave. I clear my throat, she halts and turns back to me with a bright smile on her face.

"Love you, Daddy." I'll never tire of hearing her say those words.

"I love you too, my little beauty." She quickly rushes from the room, closing the door behind her. I try to reach around Bella to grab my mouse so I can bring up the cameras to see the little shit that is taking my daughter out but Bella blocks me, earning a growl.

"Bass, she is just going to the movies with a *friend.*"

I huff and slouch back in my chair. She smiles and runs her hands through my hair. I reach up to cup her face but she snakes her hand out and grips my wrist pinning me with a look. I sigh and splay my fingers wide so she can read the tattoo's on my fingers that I got for her. On each of my fingers it reads, *my love, my life, my wife, Bella.* Marrying her thirteen years ago was the best decision I ever fucking made. Each day I make sure I show her how much I fucking love her.

"I still don't know how I managed to get you to fall in love with me, but I will spend the rest of my life being grateful that you do love me." Her body softens and melts into me.

"It was your cock that had me falling head over heels in love with you." I grin as I reach for the switch under my desk, within a second the shutters are drawn and the lights go out bathing us in blackness. Even after all these years, she still loves it when I come for her in the darkness. My hunger for her hasn't lessened over all these years, if anything it has only grown. Seeing her round with my child, I couldn't keep my hands off her for more than ten minutes before I was inside her again. Just the thought of her pregnant has my cock rock-hard beneath her. We have only started trying again this past year because it has taken that long for me to get shit with the families sorted and the handover completed.

After Audrey was born I knew that my life was with my own family and I could never risk either of my girls. I've worked my ass off for ten years in order to appoint Chip as the head and still be able to own the merc company and ensure that my family would still be taken care of even with me stepping down. Chip has made sure that happens, he is fucking thriving as the head of the family. Unlike him, I hated dealing with people constantly and always being out of the house, never being able to be home with my girls. It was an easy choice for me to hand it over to him.

"Want to know a secret?" she whispers. I grip the hem of her shirt and tug it over her head, then bury my face in her tits, moaning.

"Yeah," I growl as I reach around her and unclasp her bra, loving the way her full tits spring free. I suck her nipple into my mouth.

"Fuck!" she cries out. I swap sides and love the way she grinds down on my cock. She pulls free of my hold and stands before me as she quickly pushes her shorts down her legs, no panties like always—I fucking love that. I unsnap my jeans and push them down my legs. "Get rid of the shirt." I do as she says and wait for her to climb back on me. She presses up on her toes as I line my cock up with her entrance, then she slowly sinks down onto me.

"Fuck, Beauty," I grit out. She fucking loves working me

into a frenzy and taking her time sitting on my cock. I grip her waist and slam her down onto my cock. "Yes!"

"Fuck!" we both cry out in unison. I feel smug that I got my way. "You need to be careful doing that." I lean forward and nip at her neck loving the whimpers it draws from her.

"Why the fuck would I be careful with you, Beauty, you love it when I fuck you so hard you can't walk." She groans at my words as she begins to move, gripping the tops of my shoulders, using them as leverage as she begins to bounce up and down on my cock.

"Because I would hate for your cock to punch our baby in the head as he or she grows." I moan as she slams down on my cock ready to thrust inside her again until her words register. I grip her waist and hold her still, I can see her smile in the darkness.

"We're having another baby?" I rasp out.

"Yeah, Bass. Your beastly sperm managed to get me twice." My eyes open so wide they begin to water.

"Say what now?" She grips my face and kisses me as she begins to ride my cock, causing my thoughts to be scrambled. She breaks the kiss after a minute moaning loudly. I feel her pussy begin to squeeze my cock and growl. "Tell me," I grit out as I try to slow her movements but it's too late, we're both too far gone. I continue to thrust inside her until she comes, screaming my name. I follow a minute later, roaring her name as I come deep inside her greedy little cunt. She slumps forward, resting her face in the crook of my neck. The only sounds that can be heard in the room is our heavy breathing.

"We're having twins, Bass," she whispers. I push her back until I'm cupping her face.

"Really?" I can hear the longing in my own voice. I don't fear the thought of having children anymore, knowing that the arranged marriage rule was overturned years ago by me and her grandfather. Audrey, and now my twins, will be free to marry whoever the fuck they like.

"Yeah, Bass." I kiss her long and hard only breaking apart when the need for air overcomes me.

"I love you. Beauty."

"And I love you, my Beast."

THANK YOU!

Dear lord have mercy, how was that? You fell for the beast, didn't you?

Don't worry because I sure as fuck did as well.

Thank you so much for reading Beast and Bella's story it means a lot to me that you took a chance on this twisted retelling. I fell in love with both of these tortured souls and love how they fought for each other, Bella is a badass and I am in awe of her. The beast coming out of the shadows for the woman he loves had me swooning and falling in love with him all over again.

From the bottom of my heart thank you so so so much for reading Condemned Beast it means the world to me!

If you loved Condemned Beast, please leave a review on Amazon, Bookbub or Goodreads.

Reviews are like tips for us authors, the more reviews we get the more exposure the book gets.

Also By Samantha Barrett

Mafia Romance

<u>Murdoch Mafia Series</u>

<u>Played By The Bishop</u>

<u>Tormented By The King</u>

<u>Tortured By The Knight</u>

<u>Tempted By The Queen</u>

<u>Turned By The Pawn</u>

<u>Ruined By The Rook</u>

<u>Murdoch Mafia Novella</u>

<u>Stalemate</u>

<u>Memento Mori Series</u>

<u>Reign Of Royal</u>

<u>Broken By Sin</u>

<u>In Havoc Lays Chaos</u>

<u>Godfathers of the night</u>

<u>London has Fallen</u>

<u>Damned By His Angel</u>

<u>Re Della Strada</u>

<u>Shattered Soul</u>

Fractured Heart

Tainted Essence

<u>Fairytales With A Twist</u>

Condemned Beast

Secret Society/ Bully

Filthy Few

Forever Filthy

Filthiest Of Them All

Sports Romance

<u>Playing For Keeps</u>

Offside

Touchdown

End Game

Hail Mary

Blindside

RH Sports

Hate Us Like You Mean It

MM

Love Me Like You Mean It

Paranormal Romance

<u>The Dream Series</u>

A Beautiful Dream

A Twisted Fate

<u>A Beautiful Nightmare</u>

<u>Redemption</u>

<u>Anarchy</u>

<u>Brutal Savages</u>

<u>Savage Lies</u>

<u>Brutal Truth</u>

<u>Savage Beast</u>

<u>Brutal Beauty</u>

ACKNOWLEDGMENTS

For my *beast*, Marcus, this is the first book I have ever written where you have been the driving force behind the MMC. Beast has so many of your traits and loves just as deeply as you, if you feel the need to fuck me over a table or buy me a library, I'm good with that big boy.

My Beta girls, I love you and appreciate you so much. I love how you ladies stroke my ego and keep me humble. Clare, Sarah, and Tash, I love you!

My ARC girls, damn babes you ladies are just fucking everything! When the self-doubt kicks in you ladies make me believe in myself just from your words of love and support. Honestly, I am so blessed to have a team as amazing as you, I couldn't do this without you ladies!

A special shout out to my girl Jaye for hooking me up with this amazing as fuck opportunity to be a part of this series of retellings. I had the best freaking time writing this book and to be able to smash it out in five days was epic!

My beautiful editor Lizz, you are way too good to me. On top of rushing this edit for me because of my crazy ass deadline you still managed to edit Offside and Touchdown and never once complained. I love you and am so grateful that, Alex introduced us.

My daughter, my mini me, my terror. I fucking hope you
don't find this retelling of your favourite Disney movie until
I am six feet under and don't have to see the horrified look
on your face! My son, you are my absolute favourite guy in
the whole world and I hope to God that you never find this
book or any of the others because no son needs to read what
his mother writes!

My Kimmy, you inspired me to write the dirtiest book I
have ever written because bitch you a ho! No, I'm kidding,
you know I love ya more than you love botox.

My readers,
Thank you so much for taking a chance on little ole me and
reading this book. It means more than you will ever know. I
love you.

Sam xxx

ABOUT THE AUTHOR

Samantha Barrett is originally from Auckland, New Zealand but now lives in Brisbane, Australia.

Sam writes all things dirty dark and delicious with a side of twisted mind fuck.

She is a lover of all things red flags and an anti-hero is a must.

www.ingramcontent.com/pod-product-compliance
Lightning Source LLC
Chambersburg PA
CBHW060554190726
48283CB00003B/1010